HIS
LOST-AND-FOUND
BRIDE

HIS
LOST-AND-FOUND
BRIDE

BY

SCARLET WILSON

MILLS &
BOON

First published in Great Britain 2015
By Mills & Boon, an imprint of HarperCollins*Publishers*
1 London Bridge Street, London, SE1 9GF

Large Print edition 2016

© 2015 Harlequin Books S.A.

Special thanks and acknowledgement are given to Scarlet Wilson for her contribution to The Vineyards of Calanetti series.

ISBN: 978-0-263-26169-1

Our policy is to use papers that are natural, renewable and recyclable products and made from wood grown in sustainable forests. The logging and manufacturing processes conform to the legal environmental regulations of the country of origin.

Printed and bound in Great Britain by CPI Antony Rowe, Chippenham, Wiltshire

This book is dedicated to my fellow authors
Susan Meier, Jennifer Faye,
Michelle Douglas, Cara Colter,
Teresa Carpenter, Rebecca Winters
and Barbara Wallace.

It has been so much fun
creating this series with you!

PROLOGUE

'*SIGNOR! SIGNOR, VENGA ORA!*'

Logan Cascini was on his feet in an instant. As an architect who specialised in restoring old Italian buildings, to get the call to help transform the Palazzo di Comparino's chapel for a royal wedding was a dream come true.

The property at the vineyard was sprawling and over the years areas had fallen into disrepair. His work was painstaking, but he only employed the most specialised of builders, those who could truly re-create the past beauty of the historic chapel in the grounds and the main *palazzo*. Most of the buildings he worked on were listed and only traditional building methods could be used to restore them to their former glory.

Timescales were tight in order to try and get the chapel restored for the royal wedding of Prince Antonio of Halencia and his bride-to-be, Christina Rose. No expense was being spared—which was just as well considering he had twenty different master builders on-site.

'*Signor! Signor, venga ora!*'

He left his desk in the main *palazzo* and rushed outside to the site of the chapel. His stomach was twisting. *Please don't let them have found anything that would hold up the build.* The last thing he needed was some unexpected hundred-year-old bones or a hoard of Roman crockery or coins.

This was Italy. It wouldn't be the first time something unexpected had turned up on a restoration project.

He reached the entrance to the ancient chapel and the first thing that struck him was the fact there was no noise. For the last few weeks the sound of hammers on stone and the chatter of Italian voices had been constant. Now every builder stood silently, all looking towards one of the walls.

The interior of the chapel had been redecorated over the years. Much of the original details and façade had been hidden. The walls had been covered first in dark, inlaid wood and then—strangely—painted over with a variety of paints. Every time Logan came across such 'improvements' he cringed. Some were just trends of the time—others were individual owners' ideas of what made the building better. In restoration terms that usually meant that original wood and stone had been ripped away and replaced with poorer, less durable materials. Sometimes the damage done was irreparable.

His eyes widened as he strode forward into the chapel. Light was streaming through the side windows and main door behind him. The small stained-glass windows behind the altar were muted and in shadow. But that didn't stop the explosion of riotous colour on the far wall.

A few of the builders had been tasked with pulling down the painted wooden panelling to expose the original walls underneath.

There had been no indication at all that this was what would be found.

Now he understood the shouts. Now he understood the silence.

Beneath the roughly pulled-back wood emerged a beautiful fresco. So vibrant, the colours so fresh it looked as if it had just been painted.

Logan's heart rate quickened as he reached the fresco. He started shaking his head as a smile became fixed on his face.

This was amazing. It was one of the most traditional of frescoes, depicting the Madonna and Child. Through his historical work Logan had seen hundreds of frescoes, even attending a private viewing of the most famous of all at the Sistine Chapel.

But the detail in this fresco was stunning and being able to see it so close was a gift. He could see every line, every brushstroke. The single hairs on Mary's head, baby Jesus's eyelashes, the downy hair on his skin, the tiny lines around Mary's eyes.

Both heads in the fresco were turned upwards to the heavens, where the clouds were parted, a beam of light illuminating their faces.

Part of the fresco was still obscured. Logan grabbed the nearest tool and pulled back the final pieces of broken wood, being careful not to touch the wall. Finally the whole fresco was revealed to the viewers in the chapel.

It was the colour that was most spectacular. It seemed that the years behind the wood had been kind to the fresco. Most that he'd seen before had been dulled with age, eroded by touch and a variety of other elements. There had even been scientific studies about the effects of carbon dioxide on frescoes. 'Breathing out' could cause harm.

But this fresco hadn't had any of that kind of exposure. It looked as fresh as the day it had been painted.

His hand reached out to touch the wall and he immediately pulled it back. It was almost magnetic—the pull of the fresco, the desire to touch it. He'd never seen one so vibrant, from the colour of Mary's dark blue robe to the white and yellow of the brilliant beam of light. The greens of the surrounding countryside, the pink tones of Jesus's skin, the ochre of the small stool on which Mary sat and the bright orange and red flowers depicted around them. It took his breath away.

He'd hoped to restore this chapel to its former glory—but he'd never expected to find something that would surpass all his expectations.

'*Signor? Signor?* What will we do?' Vito, one of the builders, appeared at his elbow. His eyes were wide, his face smeared with dirt.

'Take the rest of the day off,' Logan said quickly. 'All of you.' He turned to face the rest of the staff. 'Let me decide how to proceed. Come back tomorrow.'

There were a few nods. Most eyes were still transfixed on the wall.

There was a flurry at the entranceway and Louisa, the new owner of the *palazzo*, appeared. 'Logan? What's going on? I heard shouts. Is something…?' Her voice tailed off and her legs automatically propelled her forward.

Louisa Harrison was the American who'd inherited Palazzo di Comparino and hired him to renovate both it and the chapel back to their former beauty. She was hard to gauge. Tall and slim, her long blond hair was tied up in a ponytail and she was wearing yoga pants and a loose-fitting top. Her brow was furrowed as she looked at the fresco and shook her head. 'This was here?' She looked around at the debris on the floor. 'Behind the panelling?'

He nodded while his brain tried to process his thoughts. Louisa would have no idea what the implications of this could be.

She turned back to face him, her face beaming. 'This is wonderful. It's amazing. The colours are so fresh it's as if the painter just put down his paintbrush today. I've never seen anything like this. Have you?'

He took a deep breath and chose his words carefully. 'I've seen a few.' He gave a nod to the wall. 'But none as spectacular as this.'

She was still smiling. It was the most animated he'd seen her since he'd got here. Louisa rarely talked to the tradesmen or contractors and when she did it was all business. No personal stuff. He'd learned quickly that she was a woman with secrets and he still had no idea how she'd managed to inherit such a wonderful part of Italian history.

But her intentions seemed honourable. She'd hired him after going along with the request for a wedding venue from Prince Antonio. And with his growing reputation, thriving architecture business and natural curiosity there had been no way he'd turn down the opportunity to do these renovations.

'It will be the perfect backdrop for the wedding,' Louisa said quietly, her eyes still fixed on the fresco. 'Won't it?'

He swallowed. Exactly how could he put this?

'It could be. I'll need to make some calls.'

'To whom?'

'Any new piece of art has to be reported and examined.'

She wrinkled her nose. 'And a fresco falls under that category?'

He nodded. 'A fresco, any uncovered relics, a mosaic, a tiled floor...' He waved his hand and gave a little smile. 'We Italians like to keep our heritage safe. So much of it has already been lost.'

'And you know who to call? You can sort this all out?' He could almost hear her brain ticking over.

He gave a quick nod.

'Then I'll leave it to you. Let me know if there are any problems.' She spun away and walked to the door.

Logan turned back to the wall and stood very still as he heard the quiet, retreating footsteps. The enormity of the discovery was beginning to unfurl within his brain.

He could almost see the millions of euros' worth of plans for the prince to marry here floating off down the nearby Chiana River.

In his wildest dreams the prince might get to marry his bride with this in the background. But Italian bureaucracy could be difficult. And when it came to listed buildings and historic discoveries, things were usually painstakingly slow.

He sucked in a deep breath. The air in the chapel was still but every little hair stood up on his arms as if a cool breeze had just fluttered over his skin. He knew exactly what this fresco would mean.

He knew exactly who he would have to contact. Who would have the expertise and credentials to say what should happen next. Italy's

Arts Heritage Board had a fresco expert who would be able to deal with this.

Lucia Moretti. His ex.

CHAPTER ONE

LUCIA STARED OUT of the window, sipped her coffee and licked the chocolate from her fingers.

If her desk hadn't been on some priceless antiques list somewhere she would lift her aching legs and put them on it. She'd just completed a major piece of work for Italy's Art Heritage Board. Months of negotiations with frazzled artefact owners, restorers and suppliers. Her patience had been stretched to breaking point, but the final agreement over who was going to fund the project had taken longest. Finally, with grants secured and papers signed, she could take a deep breath and relax.

She pushed her window open a little wider. Venice was hot, even for a woman who'd stayed there for the last twelve years, and the small-paned leaded-glass window obstructed her view out over the Grand Canal. A cruise ship was floating past her window right now—in a few months these larger ships wouldn't be allowed along here any more. The huge currents they unleashed threatened the delicate foundations of the world-famous city. So much of Venice had been lost already—it was up to the present generation to protect the beauty that remained.

Her boss, Alessio Orsini, put his head around the door. His eyes were gleaming and she straightened immediately in her chair. Alessio had seen just about every wonder of the world. There wasn't much left that could make his eyes twinkle like that.

'I've just had the most interesting call.' She waved her hand to gesture him into her room, but even though he was in his late seventies he would rarely sit down.

'What is it?'

He gave a little nod. 'There's been a discovery. A new fresco—or rather an old one. Just been discovered in Tuscany during a chapel restoration. I've given him your number.' He glanced at her desk. 'Seems like perfect timing for you.'

She smiled. Alessio expected everyone around

him to have the boundless energy he had. But her interest was piqued already. An undiscovered fresco could be a huge coup for the heritage board—particularly if they could identify the artist. So many frescoes had been lost already.

It seemed as though the whole of Italy was rich with frescoes. From the famous Sistine Chapel to the ancient Roman frescoes in Pompeii.

The phone on her desk rang and she picked it up straight away. This could be the most exciting thing she'd worked on in a while.

'*Ciao*, Lucia.'

It was the voice. Instantly recognisable. Italian words with a Scottish burr. Unmistakable.

Her legs gave a wobble and she thumped down into her chair.

'Logan.' It was all she could say. She could barely get a breath. His was the last voice in the world she'd expected to hear.

Logan Cascini. The one true love of her life. Meeting him in Florence had been like a dream come true. Normally conservative, studying art history at Florence University had brought Lucia out of her shell. Meeting Logan Cascini had made it seem as though she'd never had a shell in the first place.

He'd shared her passion—hers for art, his for architecture. From the moment they'd met when he'd spilled an espresso all down her pale pink dress and she'd heard his soft burr of Scottish Italian she'd been hooked.

She'd never had a serious relationship. Three days after meeting they'd moved in together. Life had been perfect. *He* had been perfect.

They'd complemented each other beautifully. He'd made her blossom and she'd taught him some reserve. He'd been brought up in a bohemian Italian/Scots family and had often spoken first and thought later.

She'd had dreams about them growing old together until it had all come to a tragic end. Getting the job in Venice had been her lifeline—her way out. And although she'd always expected to come across him at some point in her professional life she hadn't realised the effect it would have.

Twelve years. Twelve years since she'd walked

away from Logan Cascini. Why did she suddenly feel twenty years old again?

Why on earth was he calling her after all this time?

He spoke slowly. 'I hope you are well. Alessio Orsini suggested you were the most appropriate person to deal with. I'm working in Tuscany at the Palazzo di Comparino in Monte Calanetti. I'm renovating the chapel for the upcoming wedding of Prince Antonio of Halencia and Christina Rose, and yesterday we made the most amazing discovery. A fresco of the Madonna and Child. It's exquisite, Lucia. It must have been covered up for years because the colours of the paint are so fresh.'

His voice washed over her like treacle as her heart sank to the bottom of her stomach. How stupid. Of course. Alessio had just told her he'd given someone her number. He just hadn't told her *who*.

Logan Cascini was calling for purely professional reasons—nothing else. So why was she so disappointed?

It wasn't as if she'd spent the last twelve years

pining for him. There was a connection between them that would last for ever. But she'd chosen to leave before they'd just disintegrated around each other. Some relationships weren't built to withstand tragedy.

She tried to concentrate on his words. Once she'd got over the initial shock of who was calling, her professionalism slipped back into place.

This was work. This was only about work. Nothing else.

Being involved in the discovery and identification of a new fresco would be amazing. She couldn't believe the timing. If she'd still been caught up in negotiations, Alessio could have directed this call to someone else on the team. Even though frescoes were her speciality, the Italian Heritage Board expected all their staff to be able to cover a whole range of specialities.

She drew in a deep breath. Her brain was still spinning, still processing. This was the man she'd lived with, breathed with. What had he been doing these last few years?

Her heart twisted in her chest. Was he married? Did he have children?

'Lucia?'

His voice had been brisk before, but now it was soft. The way it had been when he'd tried to cajole or placate her. Just the tone sent a little tremor down her spine.

She cleared her throat, getting her mind back on the job. She had to take Logan out of this equation. This discovery could be career-changing. It was time to put her business head on her shoulders.

'What can you tell me about the fresco?'

He hesitated. 'I almost don't know where to start.' His voice was echoing. He must be standing in the chapel now. She squeezed her eyes shut. She didn't need to imagine Logan—his broad shoulders, thick dark hair and oh-so-sexy green eyes. He was already there. Permanently imprinted from the last time she'd seen him.

After all the emotion, all the pent-up frustration and anger, all the tears, she'd been left with his face on her mind. A picture of resolve. One that knew there was no point continuing. One that knew walking away was the only way they would both heal.

She'd known he wouldn't come after her. They had been past that point. He might not have agreed but he'd realised how much they'd both been damaging each other.

The vision of him standing in the stairwell of their apartment, running his hand through his just-too-long hair, his impeccable suit rumpled beyond all repair and his eyelids heavy with regret had burned a hole in her mind.

'Just tell me what you see.' She spoke quickly, giving her head a shake and trying to push him from her mind.

He sighed. 'I can't, Lucia. I just can't. It's just too…too…magnificent. You have to see it for yourself. You have to see it in the flesh.'

Flesh. Every tiny hair on her arms stood on end. Seeing it in the flesh would mean seeing *him* in the flesh. Could she really go there again?

'Wait,' he said. She could hear him fumbling and for a second it made her smile. Logan wasn't prone to fumbling. 'What's your email address?'

'What?'

'Your email. Give me your email address. I've just taken a photo.'

She recited off her email address. It was odd. She didn't even want to give that little part of herself away to him again. She wanted to keep herself, and everything about her, sealed away. Almost in an invisible bubble.

That would keep her safe.

Being around Logan again—just hearing his voice—made her feel vulnerable. Emotionally vulnerable. No one else had ever evoked the same passion in her that Logan had. Maybe it was what they'd gone through together, what they'd shared that made the connection run so deep. But whatever it was she didn't ever want to re-create it. She'd come out the other side once before. She didn't think she'd ever have the strength to do it again.

Ping. The email landed in her inbox and she clicked to open it.

As soon as the photo opened she jerked back in her seat. Wow.

'Have you got it?'

'Oh, I've got it,' she breathed. She'd spent her life studying frescoes. Most of the ones she'd encountered were remnants of their former selves.

Time, age, environment had all caused damage. Few were in the condition of the one she was looking at now. It was an explosion of radiant colour. So vivid, so detailed that her breath caught in her throat. She expanded the photo. It was so clear she could almost see the brushstrokes. What she could definitely see was every hair on the baby Jesus's head and every tiny line around Mary's eyes.

'Now you get it,' said the voice, so soft it almost stroked her skin.

'Now I get it,' she repeated without hesitation.

There was silence for a few seconds as her eyes swept from one part of the fresco to another. There was so much to see. So much to relish. The palm of her hand itched to actually reach out and touch it.

'So, what now?'

The million-dollar question. What now indeed? 'Who owns the property?' she asked quickly.

'Louisa Harrison—she's an American and inherited the property from a distant Italian relative. She hired me to renovate the *palazzo* and chapel for the upcoming royal wedding.'

Lucia frowned. 'What royal wedding?'

Logan let out a laugh. 'Oh, Lucia, I forget that you don't keep up with the news. Prince Antonio of Halencia and Christina Rose. It's only a few short weeks away.'

'And you're still renovating?' She couldn't keep the surprise from her voice. All the Italian renovation projects that Logan had been involved with before had taken months to complete. Months of negotiation for the correct materials sourced from original suppliers and then the inevitable wait for available master craftsmen.

This time he didn't laugh. This time there was an edge to his voice. 'Yes. I have around forty men working for me right now. This fresco—it was more than a little surprise. There was wood panelling covering all the walls. Every other wall we've uncovered has been bare. We expected this one to be the same.' He sighed. 'I expected just to use original plaster on the walls. It should only have taken a few days.'

Now she understood. This discovery was amazing—but it could also cause huge hold-ups in Logan's work. She'd known him long enough to know that would be worrying him sick.

Logan never missed a deadline. Never reneged on a deal. And although she hadn't heard about this wedding she was sure it must be all over the media. If Logan couldn't finish the renovations of the church in time the whole wedding would be up in the air and his reputation would be ruined.

Not to mention his bank balance. She'd no idea who the owner was, but there was every chance she'd put a clause in the contract about delayed completion—particularly when it was so vital.

'I'll come.' The words were out before she really thought about it. She grabbed a notebook and pen. 'Give me the address and I'll make travel arrangements today.' As her pen was poised above the paper her brain was screaming at her. *No. What are you doing?*

She waited. And waited.

'You'll come here?' He sounded stunned—almost disbelieving.

Her stomach recoiled. Logan obviously had the same reservations about seeing her as she had about him. But why—after twelve years—did that hurt?

But he recovered quickly, reciting the address, the nearest airport and recommending an airline. 'If you let me know your flight details I'll have someone pick you up.'

His voice was still as smooth as silk but she didn't miss the implication—Logan hadn't offered to pick her up himself.

It didn't matter that she was alone in her office, she could almost feel her mask slipping into place. The one that she'd used on several occasions over the years when people had started to get too close and ask personal questions. When past boyfriends had started to make little noises about moving to the next stage of their relationship.

Self-preservation. That was the only way to get through this.

'I'll email you,' she said briskly, and replaced the receiver. She ignored the fact her hands were trembling slightly and quickly made arrangements on her computer. Alessio would be delighted at the prospect of a new fresco. As long as it wasn't a complete fake and a wasted journey.

But it didn't sound like a fake—hidden for years behind wood panelling in a now-abandoned private chapel. It sounded like a hidden treasure. And even though she didn't want to admit it, Logan was so experienced in Italian architecture and art he would have enough background knowledge to spot an obvious fake.

She sent a few final emails and went through to give the secretary she shared with five other members of staff her itinerary for the next few days. It was five o'clock and her flight was early next morning. She needed to pick up a few things and get packed.

She turned and closed her window. Venice. She'd felt secure here these last few years. She'd built a life here on her own. She had a good job and her own fashionable apartment. There was security in looking out her window every day and watching the traffic and tourists on the Grand Canal. The thought of heading to Tuscany to see Logan again was unsettling her. She felt like a teenager.

She picked up her jacket and briefcase, opening her filing cabinets to grab a few books. She had detailed illustrations of just about every fresco ever found. There were a few artists who'd lived in Tuscany who could have painted the fresco. It made sense to take examples of their work for comparison.

She switched on her answering-machine and headed for the door. She needed to be confident. She needed to be professional. Logan would find this situation every bit as awkward as she would.

She was an expert in her field—that's why she'd been called. And if she could just hold on to the *career-defining* thought and keep it close, it could get her through the next few days.

Because if that didn't, she wasn't sure what would.

CHAPTER TWO

LUCIA STEPPED DOWN from the chartered flight with her compact red suitcase in her hand. She'd spent most of the flight going over notes, trying to determine who the likely artist of the fresco would be.

The style was vaguely familiar. But there were a huge number of fresco artists spanning hundreds of years. Often the date of the building helped with the determination of the artist, but it seemed that Palazzo di Comparino had existed, in some state, for hundreds of years. The chapel even longer. There were a number of possibilities.

The airport in Tuscany was private—owned by some local multi-millionaire—so she was practically able to walk down the steps into the waiting car.

She gave a nod to the driver. '*Grazie*, I will be staying at Hotel di Stelle.'

He lifted her case in the trunk of the black car. 'No, *signorina*. A room has been prepared for you at Palazzo di Comparino.'

Her stomach clenched. She'd been definite about booking her own accommodation. Working with Logan was one thing, living under the same roof—even for a few days—was too much.

'No, I insist. I must stay at the hotel. Can you drop my bag there, please?'

He gave a little smile and climbed into the driver's seat. The Tuscan countryside flew past. The roads in the area were winding, climbing lush green hills, passing hectares of olive groves and vineyards, filling the air with the aroma of Mediterranean vegetation. Tuscany was known for its rolling hills, vineyards and fine wines and olive oil.

It was also unique in its representation of class. Every kind of person stayed in these hills. They passed a huge array of houses and tiny cottages dotted over the countryside. Medieval villages, castles—some ruins, some renovated—and old farmhouses crowning hilltops.

After thirty minutes the car passed an old crumbling wall and turned onto a narrow road lined with cypress trees, then rolled into the picturesque village of Monte Calanetti. Lucia put down her window for a better view. The village had two bell towers that were ringing out the hour as they arrived. There was also a piazza surrounded by small shops and businesses, cobblestoned walkways going up and down the narrow streets and a fountain where a few children were walking around the small wall surrounding it and splashing water at each other.

There was an old well on one side next to red-brick houses with gorgeous flower boxes and laundry strung overhead.

A few blue and red scooters whizzed past, ridden by young men with their trousers rolled up at their ankles and their hair flapping in the wind. Helmets didn't seem to be a priority.

She smiled. It was gorgeous. It was quaint. It could be a setting for a film. Every character that was needed was there—the small wizened woman hanging her washing from a window, the young mother hurrying past with her child, a shopkeeper standing in a doorway and a couple of young girls whispering and watching the guys zipping past on their scooters.

The car turned onto another winding road, again lined with cypress trees. It only took a few moments for the *palazzo* to come into sight.

It was a sprawling, grand building with lots of little scattered buildings around. Lucia twisted in her seat, but it wasn't until the car pulled up outside the sweeping entrance of the *palazzo* that she finally saw the building she was after on the other side of the courtyard.

An old traditional chapel. Dark stonework, arched windows and door. It had two stained-glass windows, which had obviously been added at a later date than the original build.

But before she had a chance to focus on the beauty of the building something else took her breath away.

Logan, emerging from the entrance of the chapel. It had been twelve years since she'd seen him and she hadn't quite expected the jolt that was running through her body.

He ran his fingers through his dark hair, which was still a little too long. Logan had always been stylish, had always dressed as if the clothes had been made personally for him. Today he had on cream suit trousers and a pale blue shirt, open at the throat with the sleeves pushed up. Only Italian men could get away with cream suits. She imagined his cream jacket would have been discarded somewhere inside the chapel.

It wasn't just that he'd aged well. He'd aged *movie star* well. He was still lean, but there was a little more muscle to his frame. His shoulders a bit wider, his shape more sculpted. He lifted his head and his footsteps faltered. He'd noticed her at the same time she'd noticed him, but she could bet his body wasn't doing the same things that hers was.

The car halted and the driver opened her door. There was no retreat. There was nowhere to hide.

She stared down at her Italian pumps for the briefest of seconds, sucking in a breath and try-

ing to still the erratic pitter-patter of her heart.
Thank goodness she'd taken off the stilettos.
She'd never have survived the cobbled streets
of Monte Calanetti.

She accepted the extended hand of the driver
and stepped out of the car, pulling down her
dress a little and adjusting her suit jacket. The
cool interior of the car had kept the heat of Tuscany out well. It was like stepping into a piping-
hot bath. This situation was hot enough without
the sun's intense rays to contend with.

Logan walked over. His faltering footsteps had
recovered quickly. He reached out his hand towards her. 'Lucia, welcome.'

For the briefest of seconds she hesitated. This
was business. *This was business.* She tried to
appear calm and composed, even though the
first little rivulet of sweat was snaking down
her back.

She grasped his hand confidently. 'Logan, I
hope you've been well. I take it that is the chapel?' She gestured to the building from which
he'd emerged.

Straight to the point. It was the only way to

be. She had to ignore the way his warm hand enveloped hers. She definitely had to ignore the tiny sparks in her palm and the tingling shooting up her arm. She pulled her hand back sharply.

If he was surprised at her direct response he didn't show it. His voice was as smooth as silk. 'Why don't we go into the main house? I'll show you to your room and introduce you to Louisa, the owner.'

He waved his hand, gesturing her towards the *palazzo*, and she could instantly feel the hackles rise at the back of her neck.

'That won't be necessary. I'm not staying. I've booked a hotel nearby.'

Logan exchanged a glance with the driver, who was already disappearing into the *palazzo* with her red case. 'Why don't you have some refreshments in the meantime? I'd still like to introduce you to Louisa and I'm sure you'd like to see around the *palazzo*—we've already reno-vated some parts of it, including the room Lou-isa has set aside for you.'

He was so confident, so assured. It grated be-cause she wished she felt that way too. She was trying her best to mimic the effect, but it was all just a charade. Her stomach was churning so wildly she could have thrown up on the spot. It wasn't just the intense heat that was causing little rivulets of sweat to run down her back, it was Logan. Being in his presence again after all these years and the two of them standing here, exchanging pleasantries, as if what had happened between them hadn't changed their lives for ever, just couldn't compute in her brain.

Business. She kept repeating the word in her head. She was probably going to have to keep doing this for the next few days. Whatever it took to get through them. She had to be professional. She had to be polite. The Italian Heritage Board would expect her to discuss her findings and proposals with the owner directly— not through a third party. Maybe this way she could take Logan out the equation?

She gave a nod and walked over the courtyard towards the *palazzo*. The first thing she noticed as she walked into the wide entrance hall was the instantly cool air. The *palazzo* may be hundreds of years old but it seemed as though the amenities had been updated. She gently pulled her jacket from her back to let some air circulate.

Logan showed her through to a wide open-plan sitting area. Glass doors gave a wide, spectacular view over the vineyards. She was instantly drawn to the greenery outside.

'Wow. I've never really seen a working vineyard before. This is amazing.'

A beautiful slim blonde emerged from another doorway, her hair tied in a high ponytail, wearing capri pants and a white top. She smiled broadly and held out her hand. 'Welcome. You must be Lucia. Logan told me to expect you. I'm Louisa.' She nodded to the view outside. 'And I knew nothing about vineyards either before I arrived here.'

Lucia shook her hand easily. Should she be cautious? What exactly had Logan told her?

Her eyes flitted from one to the other. Was there a relationship between Logan and Louisa? She watched for a few seconds. Logan had his hands in his pockets and was waiting in the background. He wouldn't do that if he were in a relationship with Louisa and this was their home.

Louisa nodded towards the doorway that must lead towards the kitchen. 'Can I get you coffee, tea, water or...' she gave a smile '...some wine?'

Of course. She was in a vineyard. Would it be rude to say no? She was Italian, she loved wine. But she was here for business, not pleasure. 'Just some water would be lovely, thank you.'

There was a few seconds of uncomfortable silence as she was left alone with Logan again. He moved over next to her, keeping his hands firmly in his pockets.

'How is your job at the heritage board? Do you like it?'

She gave a brief nod but kept her eyes firmly on the vineyard outside. 'It was always the kind of job that I wanted to do.' She left everything else unsaid. If things had turned out differently there was a good chance that she would never have taken the job in Venice. It would have been too far away from the life they had planned together in Florence.

Something inside her cringed. It was almost as

if she'd wanted things to turn out this way and that just wasn't what she'd meant at all.

But Logan didn't seem to notice. He just seemed more concerned with filling the silent space between them. 'And how do you like living in Venice, compared to Florence?' It was his first acknowledgement of anything between them. They'd lived together in Florence for just over a year.

Louisa came back out of the kitchen holding a glass of water. 'You've lived in Florence and now Venice? How wonderful. What's it like?'

Lucia took the water gratefully. Her throat was achingly dry. For the first time since she'd got here she felt on comfortable ground—questions about Venice were always easy to answer. 'Venice is amazing. It's such a welcoming city and it absolutely feels like home to me now. It is, of course, permanently full of tourists, but I don't really mind that. My apartment is on the Grand Canal so at night I can just open my doors and enjoy the world passing by on the water. Some nights it's calming and peaceful—other nights it's complete chaos. But I wouldn't have it any other way.'

Louisa gave a visible shudder. 'Too many people for me. Too much of everything.' She looked out over the vineyards. 'I can't imagine what this place will be like when the royal wedding takes place. There will be people everywhere.' She gave a shake of her head. 'All the farmhouses and outbuildings are being renovated too. Logan's the only person staying in one right now while we still have some quiet about the place.'

Lucia didn't smile. Didn't react. But her body was practically trembling with relief to know she wouldn't be under the same roof as Logan.

Now she might consider staying in the *palazzo* for the next couple of days.

Louisa gave her a smile. 'I intend to stay out of the way as much possible. Now, about the fresco. What happens next? You do understand that we are under an obligation to get the rest of the restoration work finished as soon as possible?'

Lucia could hear the edge in her voice. The

same strong hint that had come from Logan. She chose her words carefully. 'It all depends on the fresco itself. Or, more importantly, the artist who created it.'

'Will you know as soon as you look at it?'

She held out her hands. 'It would be wonderful if we could just look at something and say, "Oh, that's by this artist…" But the heritage board requires authentication of any piece of work. Sometimes it's by detailed comparison of brushstrokes, which can be as good an identifier as a signature—we have a specialised computer program for that. Sometimes it's age-related by carbon dating. Sometimes we have to rely on the actual date of the construction of the building to allow us to agree a starting point for the fresco.'

Louisa smiled and glanced over at Logan, who looked lost in his own thoughts. 'Well, that's easy, then. Logan has already been able to date the construction of the *palazzo* and chapel from the stone used and the building methods used. Isn't that right, Logan?'

He turned his head at the sound of his name, obviously only catching the tail end of the conversation. He took a few steps towards Lucia. 'The buildings were constructed around 1500, towards the end of the Italian Renaissance period. The fresco could have appeared at any point from then onwards.'

It didn't matter how tired she was, how uncomfortable she felt around Logan—it was all she could do not to throw off her shoes and dash across the entrance courtyard right now to get in and start examining it.

She gave a polite, cautious nod. 'I'm keen to start work with you as soon as possible, Louisa.'

Louisa's eyes widened and she let out a laugh. 'Oh, you won't be working with me.' She gestured towards Logan. 'You'll be working with Logan. I have absolutely no expertise on any of these things. I've started to call him Mr Restoration. Anything to do with the work has to be agreed with him.'

Lucia eyes fell to the empty glass on the table. Where was more water when she needed it? This was the last thing she wanted to hear.

She smiled politely once again. 'But, as the owner, I need to agree access with you and have you sign any paperwork the heritage board may require. I also need to be able to come to and from the *palazzo* at my leisure. I will be staying at a nearby hotel.'

'What? Oh, no. You're staying here. Come, and I'll show you to your room.' She was on her feet in an instant. 'We have renovated some parts of the *palazzo*, you know.' She waved her hand. 'And it will all be finished before the wedding.' As she reached the door she turned, waiting for Lucia to follow her.

The corners of Logan's lips were turning upwards.

'Ms Harrison, I really don't want to put you to any trouble. I'm more than happy to stay in a hotel and just travel to and from the *palazzo*. It will only be for a few days. I don't expect my research to take any longer than that.'

Louisa shook her head. 'Nonsense. You'll stay here. I insist. As for the paperwork, Logan will need to read that first and explain it to me. My Italian is still very rusty.'

Louisa had already started up a flight of stairs, obviously expecting Lucia to follow her. 'You're going to have a beautiful view over the vine-yard. And you're welcome to use the kitchen if you want.' She paused. 'But there's a really nice restaurant in Monte Calanetti you should try.'

She wanted to object. She wanted to get away from here. But it was important that she have some sort of relationship with the owner. And because of that the words were sticking in the back of her throat. Louisa hadn't stopped talking. She was already halfway up the stairs. It obviously didn't occur to her that Lucia might continue with her objections. 'I'm sure you'll love the room.'

Lucia sucked in a breath. She wasn't even going to look in Logan's direction. If she saw him smile smugly she might just take off one of her shoes and throw it at him in frustration. At least she had the assurance that he wouldn't actually be under the same roof as her.

Just achingly close.

'I'll be back in five minutes. I want to see the fresco,' she shot at him as she left the room.

She walked up the stairs after Louisa and along a corridor. This *palazzo* had three floors—it was unusual, and had obviously survived throughout the ages. The person who'd built this had obviously had plenty of money to build such a large home in the Tuscan hills. Even transporting the stones here must have been difficult. What with the land, and the vineyard, along with all the outbuildings she'd spotted and the chapel, at one time this must have been a thriving little community.

Louisa took her into a medium-sized room with a double bed and wooden-framed glass windows overlooking the vineyard. Everything about the room was fresh and clean. There was white linen on the bed and a small table and chair next to the window, with a classic baroque chair in the corner. A wooden wardrobe, bedside table and mirror on the wall completed the furnishings.

A gentle breeze made the white drapes at the window flap, bringing the scents of the rich greenery, grapes and lavender inside. Her red case was presumptuously sitting next to the doorway.

'I'll bring you up a jug of water, a glass and

some wine for later,' said Louisa as she headed out the door. 'Oh, and we don't quite have an en suite, but the bathroom is right next door. You'll be the only person that's using it.'

She disappeared quickly down the hall, leaving Lucia looking around the room. She sank down onto the bed. It felt instantly comfortable. Instantly inviting. The temperature of the room was cool, even though the breeze drifting in was warm, and she could hear the sounds of the workers in the vineyard.

She closed her eyes for a few seconds. She could do this. Two days tops then she could be out of here again.

Logan. Seeing him again was hard. So hard. The familiar sight of Logan, the scent of Logan was tough. She couldn't let him invade her senses. She couldn't let him into her brain, because if she did a whole host of other memories would come flooding back—ones that she couldn't face again.

This is business. She repeated her mantra once more.

The smell of the Tuscan hills was wrapping

itself around her. Welcoming her to the area. Her stomach grumbled. She was hungry, but food would have to wait. She wanted to see the fresco.

She walked over and grabbed her case, putting it on the bed and throwing it open.

It was time to get to work.

Logan had finished pacing and was waiting for Lucia to appear. He'd walked back out to the courtyard and was leaning against the side of the doorway to the chapel with his arms folded across his chest.

It was much warmer out here, but he thrived in the Italian sun.

Seeing Lucia had been a shock to the system. His first glance had been at her left hand but there had been no wedding ring, no glittering diamond of promise. He was surprised. He'd always imagined that after twelve years Lucia would have been married with children. The fact she wasn't bothered him—in more ways than one.

She'd been hurt, she'd been wounded when

they'd split. Even though it had been by mutual agreement. But he'd always hoped she'd healed and moved on. When he'd heard she was working for the Italian Heritage Board he'd assumed she'd pulled things together and was focusing on her career. Now he was suspicious she'd *only* focused on her career.

Lucia had aged beautifully. She was still petite and elegant. Her pale pink suit jacket and matching dress hugged her curves, leaving a view of her shapely calves.

And she'd kept her long hair. It was maybe only a few inches shorter than it had been the last time he'd seen her. He liked it that way. Had liked it when her hair had brushed against his face—liked it even more when her long eyelashes had tickled his cheek as she'd moved closer.

It was odd. Even though there were lots of parts of his body that could have responded to the first sight of her, it had been his lips that had reacted first. One sight of her had been enough to remember the feel of her soft lips against his, remember the *taste* of her. And as she'd stepped closer he'd been swamped by her smell. Distinctive. Delicious. In any other set of circumstances…hot.

But not in these circumstances. Not when delays on this project could result in a late completion penalty that could bankrupt his company. Louisa was serious about this place being ready for the royal wedding. She was depending on it.

He straightened as Lucia appeared, walking briskly across the courtyard. She'd changed and was now wearing flat shoes, slim-fitting navy trousers, a pale cream top with lace inserts on the shoulders and a dark silk scarf knotted at her neck. She had a digital camera in her hand.

He was disappointed that her legs were no longer on display.

She stopped in front of him, meeting his gaze straight on. She'd changed a little over the years. There were a few tiny lines around her eyes, but the rest of her skin was smooth. She, like him, had naturally olive Italian skin. Her dark brown gaze was uncompromising. 'Show me your fresco, Logan.'

It was the most direct he'd ever heard her. He

tried not to smile. Twelve years had instilled a new-found courage in her. He liked it.

But something else swamped him for a few seconds. There had been a time in his life that Lucia had encompassed everything for him. She'd been the centre of his universe. He shifted self-consciously on his feet. He'd never felt that way again—he'd never *allowed* himself to feel that way again.

It was too much. Too much to have so much invested in one person when your life could change in an instant and everything come tumbling down around you both.

It didn't matter that seeing Lucia again after all these years was swamping him with a host of memories. It was time to put all those feelings back in a box. A place where they were best left.

He gestured towards the entranceway. 'It's all yours. Let's go.'

She walked ahead of him, her tight bottom right in his line of vision. He lifted his eyes to look straight in front of him and smiled as her footsteps faltered as she saw the fresco.

'Oh…whoa.'

He smiled as he stepped alongside her. 'Pretty much what I said too.'

She lifted her camera then put it back down and walked right up to the wall. She lifted her hand but didn't actually touch it. 'It's been covered for…how long?'

Logan shook his head, his hands on his hips. 'I couldn't say for sure.' He pointed to the corner of the room where debris was stacked. 'The wood panelling could be between three and four hundred years old.'

She glanced at the wood and turned back to the fresco. This time she did lift her camera and started snapping, first capturing the full work then systematically snapping detailed sections. Images that she could take time to pore over later.

When she finished she placed the camera on the floor then picked up some tiny fragments of clay that were on the floor—obvious remnants from the uncovering of the fresco. She gathered them in little plastic bags, labelled them, then put them in her bag. Once she'd finished she moved so close to the fresco that her nose was only inches away.

She lifted her fingers. It was obvious she was itching to touch it, but, she was resisting the temptation. 'I can see the movement,' she said quietly. 'I can see the brushstrokes. What kind of brush do you use to paint individual hairs? This is amazing.'

Logan waited, watching her relish her first viewing of the fresco. It was strangely exhilarating. He could see the wonder on her face, see the excitement in her eyes. Just watching her sent a little buzz through his body. Memories were sparking. This was part of the Lucia he'd loved. The wonderful, passionate girl who'd embraced life to the full. When they'd first met she'd been quiet, reserved as a result of her upbringing. But studying in Florence had made her blossom into the beautiful woman he'd quickly grown to love. The buzz, culture and bright lights had been a nurturing environment for the young artistic woman. And the two of them meeting had seemed to spark her even further. All his first memories of Lucia had been about their drive, their passion and their instant connection.

He could feel it even now—twelve years on. The palms of his hands were actually itching to reach out and touch her—just the way hers were obviously itching to touch the fresco. Parts of Lucia had been so easy to read.

Other parts she'd kept tightly locked up and tucked away. Those had been the parts that had sealed the end of their relationship. Every person grieved differently. But Logan just couldn't understand why she'd been unable to talk to *him*, why she'd been unable to share with *him*. After all, he'd been going through exactly the same thing.

He took a deep breath. 'What do you think?'

'The fresco was prepared in sections. *Giornate*—done on a daily basis with small sections of plaster laid at a time to be painted—much in the same way that Michelangelo carried out the work at the Sistine Chapel.'

Logan was incredulous. 'You think this was done by Michelangelo?'

She laughed. 'Oh, no. Of course not. The artist

of the time just used the same techniques. Michelangelo used different skin tones from those used here.' She leaned back critically. 'Different draping of the clothes. This definitely isn't his work.'

She finished snapping a few more shots with the camera and turned to face him again. 'I have a program on my computer that I can upload these pictures to. It finds similarities between frescoes and gives the most likely artists.'

He shook his head. 'Why do I feel as if you don't really need it? What's your gut instinct?'

She shook her head. 'I'm not sure. It could be one of a few possibilities.'

He pressed her again. 'But you think...' He let his answer tail off.

She brushed her hair off her shoulder. 'I think there's a chance it's a lesser-known Renaissance painter. His name was Burano.' She gave a wry smile. 'The same as one of the islands in the Venetian lagoon.'

Logan's brow creased. 'He was from Venice, then?'

She nodded.

'So what was he doing in Tuscany?'

She turned back to face the fresco. 'That's my question too. That's why I'm hesitant. I could be wrong. Journeying between Venice and Tuscany in Renaissance times wasn't easy, but we both know the European Renaissance started in Tuscany and centred in Florence and Siena.' She raised her eyebrows. 'Venice was the late starter.'

She walked back to the entranceway. 'Give me some time to run the program and see what it comes up with.'

Logan held out his hand as she made to leave. 'And in the meantime?' He spun around. 'Time is marching on, we've still got work to do in the chapel—even if we aren't anywhere near the fresco.'

She looked around and gave a little nod. 'Let me give you some recommendations on the best way to protect it in the meantime from dust, plaster and paint.' Her gaze connected with his. 'This could be a really amazing discovery, Logan.'

It was the way she'd said his name. Her accent,

her lilt. He'd heard it on so many occasions. Last thing at night, first thing in the morning. In the heat of passion and in the depths of despair.

He just hadn't admitted how much he actually missed it.

His feet were rooted to the spot. But Lucia's weren't. She was headed out the door. She was leaving. Who knew how long she would actually stay here. He could get up tomorrow morning and discover her gone.

'Have dinner with me?'

'What?' She stopped. She looked shocked.

'Have dinner with me,' he repeated, stepping closer to her. The words had come out of nowhere. He couldn't take them back. He didn't *want* to take them back.

'We have things we need to discuss.' He saw a wave of panic flit across her eyes. '*Business* we need to discuss.'

'Oh, of course.' She glanced down at her digital camera. 'My program will take a few hours to run.' She was stalling. Of course she was. The last thing she'd want to do was have dinner with him.

'Then you'll have a few hours to kill,' he said quickly. This was embarrassing. Logan Cascini wasn't used to women saying no to him. But Lucia wasn't just any woman. Lucia was the woman he'd once loved. Sure, it felt awkward. Sure, this wasn't an ideal situation.

But this was the first time he'd seen her in twelve years. If this fresco turned out to be important, it could have significant repercussions for his business. He had to keep on top of this.

He almost laughed out loud. His mind was giving him all the rational, professional reasons for having dinner with Lucia. But his heart was giving him a whole host of completely irrational, emotional reasons for having dinner with Lucia.

None of them professional. All of them personal.

His mouth kept talking. 'We can discuss any paperwork that will need to be completed. I'll need to translate everything for Louisa, and if there's going to be any extra expenses we'll need to discuss those too. There's a nice restaurant in Monte Calanetti. It will give you a chance to see the village.'

She was hesitating, looking for a reason to say no, and he wasn't prepared to accept that.

He walked around her in long strides. 'Leave the arrangements to me.'

'Well, I…I…' She was still murmuring while he left.

CHAPTER THREE

FOUR DIFFERENT OUTFITS. That's how many she'd tried on. She hadn't brought that many clothes as she'd only expected to be here a few days and hadn't expected to be socialising at all, let alone socialising with the man she used to live with. Two suits, one pair of trousers, one extra skirt and a variety of tops were all that her trusty red case held.

A white shirt, a pale pink shirt and a bright blue one were currently lying on her bed. She was wearing a flared white skirt and red shirt. And against all her better judgement a bright red pair of stilettos.

The shoes gave some height to her diminutive stature. Right now she was praying that the restaurant wasn't in the middle of the cobbled streets of Monte Calanetti.

Logan was waiting outside for her in an idling

car. She'd expected him to drive something black and sleek but instead he was in a four-wheel drive.

He gave her a nod as she opened the door and climbed in. Catching sight of her shoes, a glimmer of a smile appeared on his face. 'We're going to the local restaurant—Mancini's. I hope you like traditional food.' His eyes were gleaming.

She was nervous. And she couldn't quite work out why. Logan had changed into a white open-necked shirt and dark fitted trousers. His dark hair still had that rumpled look that she'd always loved. It was like a magnet—all she wanted to do was lift her hand and run her fingers through it.

She shifted her legs nervously in the car, crossing them one way then the other. If he noticed he didn't say anything. She eyed her shoes warily. 'Where is the restaurant?'

Logan was completely cool. He didn't seem at all unsettled at being around her. 'It's a converted farmhouse on the edge of the village. The chef's family have owned the restaurant for years, his wife-to-be is the maître d'—she's from the US.' He gave a little smile. 'It's an explosive combination.'

With Logan this was all about business. She would clearly have to adopt the same attitude.

He pulled up outside the restaurant, switched off the engine, and before she even had a chance to think he had come around the car and was opening her door and holding out his hand towards her.

She stared at his tanned hand and fingers. *Touch him.* She'd done it once. Her palm had burned for around an hour afterwards. Did she really want to touch Logan Cascini again?

How on earth could she say no?

She placed her hand in his. The sparks didn't fly this time. Probably because she was a little more prepared. This time it was a warm buzz, a little hum running up her arm and straight across to her heart.

Twelve years on, and he could still do it to her.

It was unnerving. She could hardly keep her thoughts straight.

The first glimpse of Logan had sent tingles

around her body. But that had been quickly followed by a rush of emotions associated with bad memories. Memories that were locked away deep inside her.

There was a reason she wasn't happily married with a family. There was a reason she always backed off when a few dates started to turn into something else.

Professionally, her life was good. She had a gorgeous apartment, a motivating and challenging job, along with a whole host of good friends and colleagues.

That would be enough for most people. That *should* be enough. And right up until she'd glimpsed Logan again it had been.

Now she felt…unbalanced.

She walked into the farmhouse converted into a restaurant. Thankfully there were no cobbles outside and the added height from her stilettos seemed to buffer her confidence a little.

It was cute. There were shutters on the windows and exposed brickwork on the walls. Wooden tables filled the dining room, but they weren't all uniform, like in most restaurants.

They were all different shapes and sizes, perfect for all numbers of guests, and it gave an old-world charm to the place.

They were shown to their table and the waiter lit the candle, then handed over the wine list. He nodded at Logan and pointed to the back wall. 'As you can see, we have a wide variety of wines from all the local vineyards. If you need a recommendation just let me know.'

Lucia ran her eyes down the list and sighed. Italians were passionate about their wine and the wine list was thicker than the actual menu.

'What's your preference?'

Couldn't he remember? Had he forgotten everything about their time together?

Before she had a chance to speak he waved to the waiter. 'Can we have some bread, olives and some oil while we decide?'

The waiter gave a nod and disappeared. It seemed he hadn't quite forgotten everything after all. Lucia had always enjoyed taking her time to peruse a menu, and Logan had always been starving.

She swallowed, her fingers drifting back to

the file she'd brought with her. This made it seem more real. This was work. The reason she'd agreed to dinner tonight.

She licked her lips. Nerves were doing strange things to her. 'I think I'd like to keep things simple. I'd like to have some white wine, I think, something light. A *frascati*.'

She knew he'd be surprised. During their time together they'd both favoured red wines, Merlots and Chiantis.

'And I like the look of the set menu. Sometimes it's nice to have someone else pick for you.'

She'd only glanced at the set menu and nothing had jumped out at her. Most restaurants offered a set menu of some of their best dishes. She only hoped Mancini's was the same.

In years gone by she'd been picky about her food, sometimes refusing to go to some restaurants if they didn't serve a particular dish that she liked. But she wanted to start this meeting by letting Logan realise that he didn't really know her any more. Just because he was working on this project it didn't mean that he'd get any special treatment. And she wasn't swayed by a royal wedding either.

She took her job seriously. If the fresco had been by Michelangelo everything would have ground to a complete halt. She was fairly certain it was by a lesser-known artist—one who was still recognised and his work would be protected. But the chapel was fairly well maintained. There was no damp, no immediate threat to the fresco—just the new work that was going on to make it ready for the wedding.

Once the identification part was done, things should be fairly straightforward.

Logan set his menu on the table. 'Both are fine with me.' He had a hint of a smile on his face. As if he knew she was trying to be different but it was all really just a pretence. 'How have you been, Lucia?' he asked huskily. That voice. That accent. Little waves were rolling down her spine. It was the memories. It was anticipation of what had used to come next when Logan had spoken to her like that.

Those days were long gone. Vanished for ever. It didn't matter that the words were bland and perfectly normal. It was the *way* he said them that counted.

'Twelve years is a long time, Logan.' Her voice was sharp.

He waited a few seconds before answering. His voice was low. 'You're right. It's been a very long time. Almost a lifetime ago.'

What did that mean? That for him it was gone, forgotten about? How could anyone forget losing a child? She could feel herself bristle.

'How have you been?' She bounced the question back to him. Her insides were curling up in case he told her—even though he didn't wear a ring—that he was indeed married with a houseful of children.

He nodded slowly. 'I've been busy. Building your own business takes time.' He shrugged. 'Nearly all of my time. I like to be on-site for the restoration projects. I like to make sure that everything is going to plan.'

She felt her shoulders relax a little. 'You don't like to sit in your office and drink coffee?' It was something they used to joke about years ago. Creative people ending up in jobs behind desks, drinking endless cups of coffee.

He gave a smile and shook his head as the waiter approached again, taking their order and returning a few moments later to pour the wine and leave the bread, olives and oil on the table.

Lucia took a sip. The first taste was always sharp. The second much more pleasing as her taste buds adjusted.

'Where are your offices?'

He tasted his wine too and nodded in approval. 'Florence. But I don't spend much time there.'

She tried not to raise her eyebrows. Office space in Florence was expensive. His business had obviously done well. 'Do you still live in Florence?'

He hesitated a second. And she wondered if she'd just stepped over some invisible barrier. They'd lived in Florence together. But she didn't expect him still to be in the small one-bed-roomed flat a few minutes from the university.

He nodded and dipped a piece of bread in the oil. 'I have an apartment overlooking Piazza Santa Croce.'

'Wow.' She couldn't help it. It was one of the main areas of Florence. Apartments there weren't cheap and although the existing buildings were old, they'd usually been refurbished to a high standard, hence the expensive price tags.

She gave a little nod of her head. 'I can see you staying there. Did you get to renovate the place yourself?'

He shook his head. 'If only. The apartment was renovated before I got there. But all the original architecture is still there. That's what's important.'

'Do you like staying there?' She was dancing around the subject that was really in her mind. *Did anyone stay there with him?* It shouldn't matter to her. Of course it shouldn't. But she couldn't help but feel a natural curiosity. And there was no way she would come right out and ask the question.

'It's fine. It's Florence.' He looked at her carefully. 'I've always loved living in Florence. I just don't get to stay there as much as I would like.'

'Really? Why not?' *Because your wife and child stay somewhere else?*

He shrugged. 'I've spent the last ten years building up my business. I go wherever the work is. It takes time, energy and commitment. When I'm doing a restoration—like now—I like to be on-site. I've stayed in my apartment probably only three months of the last year.'

'I see,' she said quietly, as the waiter appeared and placed their starters in front of them—wild mushroom ravioli with butter and Parmesan sauce. She was glad of the distraction. Glad to stop being watched by those too-intense green eyes.

It made sense. Logan had always been passionate about everything he'd been involved in. From his work, to his family, to his relationships. But it sounded very much like he didn't have anyone back in Florence to worry about.

'How are your family in Scotland?' she asked.

He smiled. 'They're good. They have three restaurants in Glasgow now. The one in George Square is still the main one and my *nonna* refuses to get out from behind the bar. She still sits there every day and criticises what everyone else does.'

Lucia laughed. She'd met his *nonna* on a few occasions. She was fiery little woman who was both fiercely protective and critical of her family.

'They still ask after you,' he said quietly.

Her laughter died and she swallowed quickly. There was a little tug at her heartstrings. Although both families had roots in Italy, Logan's family were much more welcoming and outgoing than her own. She'd felt more at home in their house in Glasgow than in her own mother and father's house in the small town of Osimo.

She didn't reply. She couldn't reply. Too many memories were starting to flood back. This was the problem with seeing Logan after all this time. All the things she'd literally pushed to the back corners of her mind were starting to poke their way through again.

But it wasn't just unhappy memories that were crowding her thoughts. Logan had other little places in her mind. Just sitting here with him now made a little warm glow spread throughout her body. His eyes, his accent, the way he ran his fingers through his hair when he was searching for the right words. Beautiful, sunny days in Florence, long afternoons drinking endless cups of coffee and dusky evenings with wine leading to long nights together.

Passionate. Intense. The two words that sprang to mind to describe their relationship. The third word was tragic. But she didn't even want to go there.

She was still toying with her food, wondering if either one of them would bring up the elephant in the room.

But Logan wasn't ready to go there yet. 'What do you think of Louisa?'

She put down her knife and fork. It was a curious question. The Logan she used to know would size someone up in a matter of minutes. The fact he was asking about Louisa meant he obviously wasn't quite sure.

She frowned. 'I'm not sure. I haven't really had a chance to talk to her yet. She's American, isn't she? How did she manage to own a vineyard in Tuscany?'

'From what I know, she inherited it. She's the last living relative of Signor Bartolini. It seems she might have inherited some time ago but has never visited before. As far as I can make out, Nico—who owns the neighbouring vineyard and who was a friend of Signor Bartolini—has kept it semi-functioning for the last few months. But I'm not entirely sure that Nico and Louisa have hit it off.'

She nodded thoughtfully. She hadn't met Nico yet but had heard him yelling instructions to some of the vineyard workers. He was obviously intent on keeping the vineyard working.

Logan took a sip of his wine. 'How do you find Venice?'

'It took a little getting used to. Florence was always busy, but Venice is off the scale. Cruise liners come in every day and the Piazza San Marco is so busy you can barely move.'

He gave a little nod. 'Where are you staying?'

'I was lucky. I managed to get an older apartment—much like you—on the Grand Canal. My building and street are off the main thoroughfare, but any time of the day or night I can open my doors and look out over the canal. There's never a quiet moment out there.'

'Do you live alone?' She sucked in a breath but couldn't help the amused smile that appeared on her face. It seemed that Logan didn't mind being direct. She'd skirted around the issue but he had no intention of doing that.

A tiny little part of her wanted to lie. Wanted to tell him she had a billionaire husband and three perfect children at home. But she had never been a person to tell lies. Her secret hopes and desires for her own life were just that—secret.

'Yes. It's just me. I lived with someone for a while but things didn't work out. I was consumed with work and didn't really have time for a relationship. It turned out he really didn't want a career woman for a wife anyway.'

She said the words flippantly, not giving away how much it had hurt at the time. But time, in some cases, gave a chance for reflection. That relationship would have always come to an end.

Logan's eyebrows had risen as she'd been speaking. Wasn't she supposed to move on?

But it seemed he'd opened the door now and given her a right to ask whatever she wanted.

'Why haven't you got married and settled down?' she asked.

The waiter appeared, clearing one set of plates and setting down their main course—Tuscan veal chops with Parmesan *tuilles*. The smell drifted up around her. She picked up her fork and sighed. 'This is the kind of thing I wish I had the time and talent to make.'

'Your cooking talents haven't improved with age?' He laughed. Lucia's cooking attempts had been a constant source of amusement for them. She'd once declared she could burn water—and she probably could.

The initial preparation and cooking attempts hadn't been a problem. Distraction had been the problem. Something else had always managed to crop up while she was supposed to be watching a timer or stirring a pot.

'How have you survived without someone to feed you?'

She gave a resigned nod of her head as she tasted some of the succulent veal. 'I eat out. A lot. The kitchen and I will never be friends.'

He laughed. 'I should get Nonna to package up some food for you.'

She waved her fork at him. 'Nonna should package up food for the world. She could make a fortune if she released a recipe book, or sold them to a food manufacturer.'

Logan's eyes connected with hers. 'You really expect Nonna to reveal her secret family recipes to an unsuspecting world?' He was teasing. She could tell. This was the way it used to be with them. Constant joking back and forth.

She shrugged. 'I'm just saying you have an untapped family fortune out there. That could be your nest egg, you know.'

He shook his head. 'I don't think I'd live to tell the tale.'

'Probably not.' She took a sip of her wine. This wasn't quite as bad as she'd feared. Logan wasn't being difficult, he was his usual charming self. She'd just forgotten how hypnotic those green eyes could be. Every time his gaze connected with hers she had to blink to remind herself to breathe.

Logan had always been charming. His family had joked he could charm the birds from the trees and the gods out of Olympus. And she'd loved it. She'd loved the way he could make her feel like the most important woman on the planet. Because even though Logan had been a charmer, he'd also been a one-woman man. He'd never shown a glimmer of interest in anyone else when he'd been with her. She'd felt assured in his love.

It had been a long time since she'd felt so cherished.

A little warm wave rushed over her skin as she smiled at him and took another sip of her wine. She was relaxing more as the night went on, remembering the good times instead of the bad.

Logan didn't deserve the negative associations that she'd built up in her brain. He deserved much more than that.

But if that was how she remembered him, how did he remember her?

This was more like the Lucia he'd once known. It was the first time he'd seen a genuine smile since she'd got here. When she'd walked outside to meet him earlier his heart rate had rocketed. With her perfect hourglass figure, the white flared skirt, fitted red shirt and silk scarf knotted around her neck she'd looked like a nineteen-fifties movie star. As for those killer red stilettos...

With her tumbling locks and red lips her picture could have adorned a thousand walls. His fingers couldn't decide whether they wanted to unknot the scarf around her neck and pull it free, or run down the smooth skin on her tanned legs towards those heels.

Lucia. It was odd. She tried to act so independent, so aloof, but there was an inherent vulnerability about her that made him lose focus on everything else. He felt strangely protective and proud of her. The last time he'd seen her she'd been a shell of her former self. Losing their child had devastated them both.

Although the pregnancy hadn't been planned they'd both been delighted when they'd found out a baby was on the way. They'd spent hours talking about their future together and making preparations for their baby. At one point it had seemed that the whole apartment had been full of brochures for cribs, cabinets, prams and high chairs.

The twenty-week scan had revealed a perfect daughter waiting to be introduced to the world.

No one could explain the unexpected premature labour.

No one could explain why Ariella Rose hadn't managed to take those first few vital breaths.

Of course, the doctor had tried to say that her lungs hadn't been developed enough and there had been no time to give Lucia steroids to help Ariella's lungs mature.

It had been that terrible time when doctors tried to decide if a baby's life was viable or not.

Some babies did breathe at twenty-three weeks.

Ariella Rose hadn't.

The beautiful, vivacious woman he'd known had disintegrated before his eyes, their relationship crumbling around him. He'd spent months desperate to get her to talk to him. But Lucia had put up walls so thick nothing had penetrated.

Every time he'd tried to draw her out of her shell she'd become more and more silent and withdrawn. He'd pulled back too, focusing on his work, because right then that had been all he'd had. But Lucia had slipped through his fingers like grains of sand from the beach.

He'd been grieving too, watching the days tick by on the calendar, waiting for the day they would have welcomed their daughter into the world.

That had been the day Lucia had packed her cases and left.

No amount of pleading had dissuaded her. Florence had had too many bad memories for her—too many painful associations. She'd accepted a job in Venice. She'd wanted to leave, and she hadn't wanted him to follow.

Now his insides twisted. He'd always regretted that he hadn't fought harder. Hadn't found the words to persuade her to stay.

It was almost a relief to see her now. There was a stillness about her—something reserved that hadn't been there before they'd lost their daughter. He could still see a remnant of sadness in her eyes.

But this Lucia was different. She had a different kind of confidence around her. She was a little more self-assured. She'd been through the worst and come out the other side. There was a real resilience there that bubbled underneath the surface.

Her clothes and demeanour were back to the woman he remembered. She'd always worn her stilettos with pride, as if to take someone to task for her diminutive height. And her hair was every bit as tempting as it had always been. It had always felt like silk and smelled of roses. Even now, there was a faint floral aroma drifting across the table towards him, curling its way around him and kicking his senses into gear.

The waiter appeared to clear their plates. 'Dessert?'

'No, thank you.' They both answered in unison and Lucia threw her head back and laughed.

Now his fingers were definitely itching to reach across and tug that scarf from her neck and reveal the paler sensitive skin around her décolletage.

It was her tender spot. The area that when kissed sent her into a spin. It had always been guaranteed to make her go weak at the knees.

He shifted uncomfortably in his chair. Parts of his body were awakening that shouldn't— not in a public restaurant. 'Do you want to have coffee?'

She shook her head. 'I'm tired. I still need to do some work online.'

Work. Of course. The reason they were here. He'd barely even discussed the project with her. He was normally so pedantic about every detail of his build. It seemed that even being around Lucia for a few hours was making him lose focus.

He should be worrying about delays. He should be panicking that his business could be affected by the non-completion clause in his contract.

If things weren't ready on time for the royal wedding he might have to face the wrath of the wedding planner, Lindsay Reeves. She was already phoning him twice a day for updates and photos of the chapel.

He took a deep breath and tried to collect his thoughts. 'Can we continue our work in the chapel?'

This was useless. Now he was looking at those deep brown eyes. Lucia's eyes had always been able to draw him in completely. In twelve years they hadn't lost their magic.

People said that eyes were the window to the soul. Lucia's brown eyes were very dark, very deep and flecked with gold. He could get lost in them completely. Always had.

She blinked. 'In truth, probably not. Give me another day. I have a few ideas. If I needed to go elsewhere to verify who painted it, would you have someone who could ensure the safety of the fresco?'

He straightened in his chair. 'Why would that be needed? It's been safe for the last five hundred years beneath the panels in the chapel?'

She gave an apologetic smile. 'But now it's been discovered. Now it's open to the elements. And now we have a whole host of tradesmen who know that it exists.' She shrugged. 'What if people have thoughts like you first did? What if they think that there is a tiny possibility this could be a Michelangelo work? What if someone tells the press?'

She held out her hands. 'In the space of a few hours this whole village could be swamped by a whole host of people—not all of them with good intentions.' She spoke with complete sincerity. He'd always respected Lucia's ambition, but he was now seeing a true glimpse of her professional expertise.

He nodded slowly. 'Of course. Louisa has already expressed some concerns about publicity. She's worried enough about the royal wedding without having to deal with something else.' It was easy to know who to discuss this with. 'Connor Benson is the head of security for the royal party. He'll know exactly how to keep things safe and protect the fresco in the meantime.'

She gave him an amused smile. 'Isn't he more at home looking after real-life people than artefacts?'

Logan lifted his hands. 'He has the skill and expertise we need. What's more important is that I trust him. If he says he can keep the fresco safe, then I believe him.'

He signalled to the waiter for the bill. Lucia had told him she still had work to do. It didn't matter that he wasn't in a hurry for this evening to end. He had to respect the job she was here to do.

It only took a few minutes to pay the bill and head back out to the car. The sun was setting behind the deep green Tuscan hills, sending shards of orange and red across the sky.

Lucia took a deep breath as they stepped outside. 'How beautiful.' She spun around in her heels, her skirt swishing around her, a relaxed smile on her face.

He caught her arm as she spun, feeling her smooth skin against his palm. 'You've never experienced a Tuscan sunset. It really is something, isn't it?'

The evening was still warm and pleasant. 'Why don't we go for a walk before we head back to the *palazzo*?' The words were out before he thought about it and he could sense her immediate reluctance.

But what struck him straight away was the way his stomach curled. He hated seeing Lucia like this, prickly and difficult around him. Towards the end of their relationship she'd been so flat. Almost emotionless, as if everything had just been drained from her. It had just been another stage of grieving—he appreciated that now.

But at the beginning she'd been bright, bubbly and vivacious. He didn't know this prickly and difficult version. More importantly, he didn't know how to *act* around her.

He waved his hand. 'Of course, if you want to head straight back, that's fine. I just thought you might want to have a chance to see around Monte Calanetti a little.'

It was official.

She was caught between a rock and a hard place.

Strange as it seemed, getting a sense of the village might actually help her identify who the artist of the fresco might be. Often, if someone had stayed in an area there might be historical stories or some folklore about them. Sometimes getting a sense of a place, seeing other work done in the area could actually help. And, in some respects, Logan's brain worked exactly the same way that hers did.

She sucked in a breath, holding it for a few seconds, her eyes fixing on her red stilettos. They'd seemed like a good idea at the time. But she'd seen the streets of Monte Calanetti. Cobbles. Everywhere. She'd probably land on her back.

She bit her lip. Logan's gaze was fixed on the sunset, his face basking in the orange glow. Her reserve softened. With his dark hair, tanned skin and dark suit jacket he was definite movie-star material. Age suited him. The little lines around his eyes gave him even more charisma, and Logan had oozed it already.

'Okay, then.' *Where had that come from?*

She was almost as amazed at her words as Logan was, judging by the expression on his face. He recovered quickly. 'Great, let's go.'

He drove the car into the town centre and parked outside a bar. He walked swiftly around and opened the door, holding his hand out to her as he had before.

She didn't hesitate. Didn't think about the contact. She was making too much of this. It was probably just all in her head anyway.

Wrong move. She could almost see the spike of electricity.

One of her heels automatically slipped in a gap in the cobbles and he caught her elbow, sliding one arm behind her waist. She pretended it was nothing. Nothing—to feel his body right next to hers.

Her throat was so dry she couldn't even swallow. This wasn't supposed to happen. She was in self-protect mode.

She could smell him. Smell his woodsy aftershave, his masculine scent winding its way around her body. So familiar. So scintillating.

He slammed the car door, keeping one hand around her waist. 'Don't want you to stumble,' he said throatily.

It was an excuse. She knew it was an excuse

to keep her close. But she didn't feel in a position to protest. The likelihood of her landing on her backside had just increased tenfold. The cobbles weren't the only thing affecting her balance around here.

He steered her towards the centre of the square, near a fountain and old brick well.

Now Lucia really had a chance to see the beauty of the square, the most quirky thing being that it wasn't exactly a square. The fountain was similar to lots found in small Italian villages. Built with travertine stone, it was circular with a sleeping nymph at its centre. The old well was solid with mismatched stones. Like most of Italy's traditional village wells some modernisation had taken place and water from the well could be accessed via a pipe at the side. Logan pressed the button and reached over for her hand. She didn't have time to pull it back before cool, clear water poured over their fingers.

He lifted his hand, letting the drops fall into his mouth. Her legs quivered. She put her fingers to her lips and tasted the cold water. It was surprisingly fresh. She smiled as a drop trickled down her chin.

Logan moved instantly and caught the drop with his finger. She froze. Before it had just been touching hands, arms. Even holding her close, she was still completely clothed.

But touching her face was different. Touching her face was a complete and utter blast from the past. Logan had always touched her face—just before he kissed her.

It had been their *thing*. She'd used to close her eyes and he'd trace his finger over her skin like butterfly kisses. It had always driven her crazy.

And even though she willed it not to happen, as soon as he touched her chin her body reacted. She closed her eyes.

This was something she wasn't prepared for. This was something she'd *never* be prepared for. She sucked in a sharp breath and forced her eyes back open.

Their gazes meshed. So focused, so intense it made her want to cry.

Logan's deep green eyes were so clear, so solid. He was everything she'd ever wanted. Everything she'd ever needed. The person she'd love for ever. The person she'd never forget.

Something flashed across his vision. Panic. Something she'd never seen before in Logan's eyes. He was the calmest, most controlled man she'd ever known.

He pulled his finger back and stared at it for a second, as if he were being hit with the same overload of memories she was.

She wobbled, adjusting her weight in her stilettos. Logan blinked and lifted his hands onto her shoulders, walking her back a few steps to the edge of the fountain. She sagged down, breathing heavily, trying to ignore the pitter-patter in her chest.

She adjusted her position at the edge of the fountain and her eyes fixed on the nymph in the centre of the cascading water. It was exquisite. Serene and beautiful, holding a large clamshell above her head.

Logan stepped in front of her. She was so conscious of him, of his strong muscular thighs barely hidden inside the dark suit trousers. He didn't speak. He didn't try to touch her again.

Her brain tried to clear a little. This was ridiculous. She wasn't the young woman she'd been the last time she'd been around Logan. She'd lived and aged twelve years. Sometimes inside it felt like she'd aged another forty.

She tried to focus her attention on something else. Something safe. The sculpture of the nymph.

Most nymphs were naked. This nymph wasn't. It was clothed. In a cloak. A cloak with characteristic folds.

She straightened up.

'What is it?' Logan crouched down next to her.

She pointed to the nymph. 'Do you know anything about this?'

He touched the wall of the fountain where she was sitting. 'About the fountain?'

She shook her head. 'No. About the nymph. Do you know who sculpted it? Is there any village history that would tell us?'

His eyes were fixed on hers. 'I know the legend attached to the fountain.'

Her heart started to beat faster. 'What's the

legend?' She was watching the fine billowing mist that seemed to glow in the lowering sun. Of course. Every village fountain in Italy would have a legend.

He gave her a wistful kind of smile. 'They say that if you toss a coin and it lands in the clam-shell you get your wish.'

Her stomach clenched. It wasn't exactly what she'd wanted to hear. But it reached into her and grabbed a tiny part of her soul. Oh, she had a whole host of things she could wish for. But most of them were in the past. And nothing would change that now.

Wishful thinking. That's all that could happen around this fountain. And a fanciful legend didn't help her identify the sculptor. 'Do you know anything else? Anything more realistic?'

He looked as if he'd been stung. He frowned. 'I have no idea. Is it important?'

She stood up and spun around to face it. 'It could be. See the folds of the cloak?'

He leaned forward. 'Yes...' His voice was hesitant.

She touched his arm. 'Does it look familiar to you?'

His face broke into a smile, there was a mischievous twinkle in his eyes and he held up his hands. 'Is yes the right answer?' It was clear he had no idea.

But something had sparked a fire within her. 'I think it might. Most Renaissance artists didn't just paint—they also sculpted. It could be the nymph was sculpted by the same person who painted the fresco. The folds of the cloak are quite characteristic. If I can compare the fresco and the nymph to the works of art that are held in Venice, it could help identify the artist.'

He started to nod his head in recognition. 'You still think its Alberto Burano?'

She smiled. 'It could be.'

This was work. Work she could do. Talking about work made her feel confident again. Made her feel safe.

'So what happens now? How long will it take you to find out?'

She paused. Of course. 'These things can take weeks—sometimes months. The Italian Heritage Board is cautious. We have to be careful before we make any kind of declaration about the potential artist of any fresco. It can always be challenged by others.'

Logan shook his head. 'But what happens in the meantime? Can the wedding still go ahead in the chapel? Louisa is absolutely adamant that things must go to plan. I suspect she's counting on the money from the royal wedding to help her complete the renovations on the *palazzo*. If we can't progress...' His voice tailed off.

There were deep furrows in his brow. He put his hands on his hips and stared out across the village. It was obvious that something else was bothering him.

'If we can't progress—what?'

He let out a deep breath and turned to face her. 'We have a non-completion clause in the contract. It's standard practice in the renovation business.'

'What happens if you don't complete on time?' Now she understood why he looked so worried.

He couldn't meet her gaze. Her brain whirred. She knew exactly what would happen. Logan's company would have to bear the brunt of any costs.

Something twisted inside her. It had been a long time but Logan had been the father of her child. She knew exactly how much something like this would matter. If he failed to complete this job his reputation would be ruined—he could kiss his company and all his hard work goodbye.

'Is there anything I can do to help prevent the delays?' There was an edge to his voice. Determination.

From the second she'd got here all she'd wanted to do was get away. Being around Logan was claustrophobic, too cluttered—stifling, too many memories.

But she couldn't let his business fall apart because of things he had no control over. This wasn't his fault.

She hesitated. 'There will be a whole lot of paperwork that will need to be completed in Venice. That's always the thing that causes the most delays. If Louisa will allow you to be a signatory for her it could make things much easier. As you know, Italian paperwork can be complicated.'

'You want me to come to Venice?' He sounded a little stunned.

But so was she. Had she really just suggested that?

'Well…it might move things along more quickly. I will be working on the comparisons with other frescoes. If you could find any history of the village that might link Alberto Burano to being here it could also be a huge benefit.'

He nodded slowly. She could almost see him thinking everything over, weighing up the best way forward.

He stepped forward. A little closer than she expected and as she breathed in all she could smell was his woodsy aftershave.

'What day do you want me in Venice?' His voice was determined.

'Friday,' she said quickly, trying not to think about it too much.

Friday was only a few days away. She would have done some of the groundwork before he got there.

He seemed to wait a few seconds before he replied. His voice was low and husky, sending shivers down her spine. 'Friday it is.'

What had she just done?

CHAPTER FOUR

THE HEAT IN Venice was stifling. It seemed the whole world had descended on it to hear one of the world's biggest rock bands play in a concert. Piazza San Marco was positively heaving, the streets crowded beyond measure and tourists juggling to pay the inflated prices in the surrounding cafés and bars.

Venice was always hot in the summer and Lucia was used to it. Living in the middle of permanent tourist attractions meant it was rarely quiet but today was the busiest she'd ever seen it. The queue of people to get inside St Mark's Basilica snaked around the centre of the piazza twice.

Lucia glanced at her clock again. She'd expected Logan to call her over an hour ago. When they'd made the arrangement for him to come and help complete the paperwork she'd had no idea about the rock concert. It hadn't even been on her radar. She didn't want to think about what Venice Marco Polo Airport was like right now. She knew that the wait for the water buses was over an hour and that everything was going much slower than expected.

But the heat in her office was becoming claustrophobic. Even with her windows opened wide over the Grand Canal there was no breeze. She glanced at the clock again and pulled her fitted blouse away from her back. The air conditioning rarely worked at the Italian Heritage Board. Today was no exception.

She gathered up the papers she might need, closed her windows and headed for the door. Her mobile sounded just as she walked down the stairs. Logan. She answered quickly, but could barely make out his voice for the background noise. 'Logan, where are you?'

She walked out into the bustling crowds, her feet turning automatically in the direction of San Marco, the waterbus drop-off on the Grand Canal. His voice was lost as she struggled to hear, so she continued through the thronging crowds towards the drop-off point. There, in the distance, she could see Logan and a smile flickered to her face.

His bag was clutched in one hand, alongside a pale beige jacket and his mobile phone. His white shirt was wrinkled, his hair rumpled and his face red. It was the first time in her life she'd ever seen Logan looking hot and bothered. It was kind of nice to know that could actually happen to him too.

He ran his fingers through his hair and looked around him, scanning the crowds. The rock concert had obviously caught him equally un-awares.

She lifted her hand and waved at him, snaking her way through the people. A flash of relief was all over his face and gave her an unexpected glow. He moved towards her. 'Lucia, thank goodness.' He held up his hands. 'This place is even madder than usual. It wasn't until I hit the airport that I heard about the concert. I guess I should have got an earlier flight. The queue for the water taxis and buses was a mile long.'

She gave a nod and glanced at his bag. 'You

look hot. How about we find somewhere to sit down and get something cool to drink?'

Logan let out a long breath, his brow furrowed. 'Do you think you'll be able to find anywhere?'

Lucia gave a little nod of her head. 'You forget, Logan. I've been here more than ten years. I know all Venice's best kept secrets.' She nodded her head for him to follow and weaved through the crowds. She was glad she'd opted out of wearing her normal business attire today. In these conditions she would have sweltered in her fitted suit dress. Instead, the lighter short-sleeved white blouse and knee-length navy skirt helped to keep her cooler. She pulled her sunglasses down from her head and snaked her way through the cobbled side streets of Venice. These were instantly cooler out of the sun's blistering rays and after a few minutes' walk they were away from the madding crowds.

She pointed towards a café with tables and parasols set on the street. Logan gave a sigh of relief and sank down into a chair. 'Perfect,' he said.

The waitress appeared instantly and they both

ordered two drinks, one cool and one coffee for later.

She was still amused by how flustered he looked. 'I'm sorry about being so late, Lucia. I hope I haven't ruined your schedule for the day.'

She shook her head. 'No problem. I'd just decided to leave a little earlier because it was so hot. I'm happy to meet you outside rather than in the office.' She pulled out her files. 'I brought the paperwork with me. We can do it now, if you like.'

The waiter appeared and put their drinks on the table. Logan finished his cool drink within a few seconds, then sat back in his chair and sighed. He gave her a quirky smile and held up his hands. 'I don't remember Venice ever being this hot. What on earth is happening?'

She shrugged her shoulders. 'A cross between a heat wave and an extra twenty thousand people descending on the city at once?' She pushed the papers over towards him. 'These are the ones I need you to complete. Then we can file the fresco as a "new find" with the Heritage Board. They are the ones that can authorise any restoration that might need to take place.'

Logan was scouring the papers. He lifted his eyes towards her. 'And who would do that?'

She paused for a second, wondering if it was an answer he really wanted to hear. 'It would probably be me. I've done most of the work on all of the last frescoes that needed to be restored. It used to be my boss, Alessio Orsini, who handled fresco restoration, but once he'd trained me and overseen my work a few times he was happy to hand over the reins. I think he's looking to retire soon.'

Logan nodded slowly. He sat down his pen. 'How would you feel about working in Tuscany? There is a good chance that I'll still be there for the next few months.'

Logan was being cautious, but for some reason she felt as if a little man with icy feet was marching down her spine. It was almost as if he didn't want her there. She felt insulted.

She looked at him steadily. 'I'll go wherever I'm needed. My job is very important to me. The other personalities involved aren't important.' She picked up her cappuccino and took a sip, breaking the little caramelised biscuit at the side into pieces.

'That's not what I meant.' He reached over and grabbed her hand.

It was unexpected. A little part of the biscuit dropped from her hand onto the cobbled street.

Her eyes fixed on it lying amongst the cobbles, rather than looking at his hands or his face. She didn't pull her hand back. 'I get it, Logan. You'd rather not have to work with me. But I won't compromise on my job. We're just going to have to both be professional about it.' She lifted her gaze to meet his.

His eyes widened. 'No, Lucia. You're reading this all wrong.' He squeezed her hand. 'I know we had a difficult past. And seeing you after all these years…it's been…' He seemed to struggle to find the right word. 'It's been hard.'

She felt her heart squeeze.

He moved the position of his hand. This time his thumb was inside her palm, moving in tiny circular motions, while the rest of his hand rested over hers.

He lowered his voice. 'But it's been good to

see you, Lucia. Really good. It's left me wondering why we didn't do this earlier.'

She didn't hesitate. 'Because it would have been too hard.' Her gaze was steady on his. 'And you're right, it is still hard.'

'But it doesn't have to be?' There was an edge of optimism in his voice. A little glimmer of hopefulness.

Tears prickled in her eyes. A lump rose instantly in her throat. This was dangerous territory. Business was business, but this was something else entirely. She swallowed. 'I think it always will be. There's too many memories. Too many associations.'

He didn't move. Didn't flinch. Logan had always been like this. His thumb kept moving in little circles, the way it always had when he was trying to soothe her. And for the most part it worked. Logan had always been cool, almost like the eye of a storm. Few things made him ever raise his voice. Few things made him rattled.

She looked at him again. He was still her Logan. Still so handsome. Still so protective.

Grief had made his love feel suffocating. But the truth was Logan had never been suffocating. He'd encouraged her to blossom and grow while they'd been in Florence together. He'd be the very person to tell her never to hide her light under a bushel.

Why on earth hadn't he met someone over the last twelve years? Why wasn't he married with children? It had always been what he wanted. And he'd seemed to cope so much better with the death of Ariella Rose than she had.

He'd been grief-stricken for sure. The plans they'd made for baby furniture and paraphernalia had silently disappeared. He'd spoken to the doctors regarding a proper burial. Things were difficult when a baby was so young. But Logan's calm and assuring manner had persuaded them to go along with his wishes and they'd got to lay Ariella Rose to rest in a cemetery just outside the city walls.

The short ceremony by the priest had been beautiful, the flowers and funeral arrangements all carried out by Logan—she'd been too numb to help with any of it.

It was only now, in hindsight, that she could appreciate just how hard that must have been for him. She hadn't been the only one to cry over the death of their daughter. And after he'd spent days trying to get her talk and she hadn't responded he'd finally stopped and mirrored her behaviour. Closing in on himself and shutting out the world around him.

He finally replied. 'Let's just see how things are. I'm glad we've met again, Lucia. I'm glad that you're settled in an amazing city and doing a job that you love.'

There it was. The unspoken words.

I'm glad you've finally moved on.

But had she?

All he wanted to do was reach across the table and hold her. Lucia was at her most fragile right now. He could see the hidden pain in her eyes and he hated it that he was the person who had done that to her. Hated that her association with him was her most painful memory.

He had painful memories too. But he was still able to remember the good times in Florence—

running through one of the fountains during a rainstorm, watching her face when he'd come home with every flower that the street vendor had been selling, sneaking out in the morning to buy her favourite pastry and watching her nose twitch as she'd woken up to the smell. For a long time Lucia had been his joy—and the feeling had been mutual. He only wished he was still hers.

She'd haunted his dreams on and off for years. Dreams about them meeting again in some random place, having dinner together, or catching each other's eye across a crowded room.

He'd always dreaded hearing the news that she was happily married or settled with a family of her own, but somehow seeing her like this was equally hard. More than anything he wanted Lucia to be happy.

Seeing her again was sparking a whole host of emotions that he'd long forgotten. He'd never imagined that the spark between them would still feel so electric. He'd never imagined that once he'd stared into those brown eyes again he'd feel rooted to the spot and never want to break away.

Lucia brushed her chocolate hair from her shoulder. It was a little shorter than he remembered and it suited her. She pulled her hand back steadily, keeping her gaze on his. He could almost see her retreating back into herself and putting a carefully drawn line between them.

She picked up her coffee cup. 'How soon do you think you'll get the paperwork completed?'

Business. That was all she wanted to discuss with him. Even after all this time.

He nodded, picking up the biscuit from the side of his cappuccino and placing it on her saucer. He didn't miss the little hint of a smile from her.

'How soon can you tell me I can finish my renovations?'

She blinked. 'Well…' She paused. 'Actually, I'm not sure. We have to file your paperwork, then I need to do some investigating. I've made a private appointment tomorrow to view another fresco by the artist we think is involved.'

He sat back in his chair. 'Well, that's fine. I'll come with you.'

She looked surprised. 'Why would you want to come with me?'

He shrugged. 'There's not much point in me going back if I can't give Louisa good news. She needs to know that the renovations and wedding plans can continue. At the moment most of the work in the chapel has ground to a halt. There's still work ongoing in the *palazzo* but it doesn't require my supervision every day. The chapel will be the difference between this wedding going ahead or not.'

Lucia looked thoughtful. Her fingers started twiddling with a strand of her hair and she crossed her legs, giving him a flash of her tanned skin. 'What do you know about the royal couple?'

He shook his head. 'Virtually nothing. I've mostly dealt with Lindsay, the wedding planner.' He laughed. 'Now, there's a woman I don't want to call to say there's an issue with the chapel.'

Lucia smiled. 'Will she chew you up and spit you out?' There was a little spark of amusement in her eyes. It suited her. It made her more like the Lucia he remembered. The Lucia he *wanted* to remember.

'In a heartbeat,' he said quickly. 'There's no point in going back until I know I'm safe.'

Lucia frowned. 'Where have you made arrangements to stay?'

This time he frowned too. Oh, no. 'Well, I haven't. Not yet anyway.' His brain started spinning. 'There's a small boutique hotel I stay in if I ever come to Venice. I can give them a call.' He pulled his mobile from his pocket and started dialling.

Lucia shook her head and held out her hands. 'Have you seen this place? I've never seen Venice this busy. I think everywhere will be packed out.'

So do I. He was cringing inside. He'd known as soon as he'd arrived that he would never make his flight back. It was leaving right around now. And he hadn't even made any attempt to book another. With this number of tourists he imagined that every flight and train journey, in and out of Venice, was booked for the next few days.

He pressed the phone to his ear. 'Hi, there, it's Logan Cascini. I wondered if there was any chance of reserving a room for the night.'

He listened to the reply and tried to stop the sinking feeling settling over him. 'No problem. Can you recommend anywhere else?'

The crease across Lucia's brow was deepening.

He listened to the receptionist telling him what he already knew. Venice was packed. Every hotel was fully booked for the next two days. He cut the call and gave his best attempt at a shrug. 'I'll try somewhere else.'

Lucia sucked in a breath. 'Why do you want to stay, Logan? There isn't anything that you can actually do. Did you book a flight back to Tuscany?'

Her tone was almost accusatory. He pressed a button on his phone and spun it around, showing her his online boarding card for the flight that was due to take off any minute.

Her eyes widened. 'Oh.'

She bit her lip again. 'Why do you even *want* to stay?'

The same question again. This time with a different emphasis on the words. It was obviously preying on her mind, just like it was preying on his. When he'd booked his flight he'd planned to be in Venice for four hours and leave again later today and go straight back to Tuscany. It had all seemed straightforward. Except in his mind, where a little voice kept niggling at him.

This was the contact he'd always imagined making. The renovations were a perfect excuse to be around Lucia. He hadn't planned it. It had surprised him just as much as it had surprised her. But sometimes fate had a mysterious hand in things.

After the first few awkward moments curiosity had been killing him about Lucia. He wanted to know everything about the last twelve years. He wanted to know her plans for the future. If she was happy. If she was settled.

And absolutely none of it was his business. But that didn't stop the little craving that had always been there growing into something a whole lot bigger.

There would always be something between

them. Right now, it still felt as if there was a big black cloud hanging over them. But for him, he could see little remnants of sunlight struggling to get through. And he wanted them to get through. So badly.

But still something was holding him back. Holding him back from saying their daughter's name and asking Lucia if she was ready to talk about her.

So he took the easy way out. The safest way out, if he wanted to still have contact with Lucia.

'I want to stay because I want to help move this project along. I would love to see Burano's fresco. I would love to see how it compares to the Madonna and Child and to the nymph sculpture. You know I love this stuff just as much as you do.'

Part of him felt guilty. These were careful words, designed to push the little buttons inside her and help things spark along.

There was a glimmer in her eyes. He was talking her language. A language she related to and understood.

He pulled something from his bag. 'Look at

this. You told me to try and find any evidence that Burano had been around the village. I've photocopied something from the local museum. One of the guest houses had an ancient register. People used to stay for months at a time.' He pointed to a blurred entry from 1530. 'I thought that might be Alberto Burano.'

She screwed up her nose and squinted at the blurred entry. It was difficult to judge but he could see the glimmer of excitement behind her eyes.

'I'm sure we'll have a sample of his writing somewhere at the heritage board.' She met his gaze. 'This could be really important, Logan. You did well to find this.'

It was the first note of approval he'd had from her and it made his heart swell in his chest. He wasn't going to tell how he'd had to bribe the local museum curator to let him riffle through all the old paperwork. He wasn't going to let her know he'd spent all of last night checking through mountains of ancient chests in order to find anything that might help.

'Can I take this?' she asked, holding up the photocopy.

He nodded as he zipped up his bag again.

'This can definitely help.' She looked around them. The number of people in the quiet street was starting to pick up. 'But where will you stay?'

The million-dollar question. He shrugged as he desperately tried to think of someone, *anyone* he still knew in Venice.

His fingers flicked through the numbers on his phone. He had a multitude of contacts in Florence, Rome and Pisa. Venice? Not so much.

'You can stay with me.'

The words came out of the blue. It was absolutely the last thing he was expecting to hear.

'What? No, I couldn't possibly put you to any trouble.' His stomach clenched.

He couldn't miss the expression on her face. She was saying the words, but it was reluctantly—this wasn't a warm invitation.

And he hated that. He hated that she felt obliged to offer him somewhere to stay—when it was obvious she didn't really want to.

That hurt.

But the reality was that he really didn't have anywhere else to go. Chances were he could spend the next two hours phoning every hotel and just get the same answer—fully booked. There was a strong likelihood he wouldn't find a bed for the night.

Part of him wanted to refuse graciously and just walk away.

But something else was burning inside…a persistence.

Lucia used to be his. She used to fill his whole world. And he knew that the feelings had been mutual.

They were both adults. They were twelve years away from their shared past. Determination was overcoming him.

He didn't want to walk away from Lucia—no matter how awkward she felt.

In another world she would love him just as much as she always had, and would be delighted to offer him somewhere to stay and he would be delighted to accept.

But in another world they wouldn't have lost Ariella Rose.

His fingers itched to reach over and touch her soft hand.

Her own hands were knotted together, turning over and over in her lap.

The rational part of his brain kicked in. He needed to get this job back on track. He needed to finish the renovations at the *palazzo* and the chapel.

And the history-loving part of him would love to see the other fresco. This wasn't such an unreasonable offer to accept. Another night in Venice might give him a little time to get to know Lucia again.

And it seemed as though the rest of Venice might be attending a concert somewhere, leaving the beauties of Venice still to be explored…

He lifted his gaze to meet hers. 'Thank you, Lucia. You're right. I probably won't be able to find anywhere else to stay. As long as you're sure it's not too much trouble, I'd be delighted to stay.'

CHAPTER FIVE

WHAT HAD SHE just done?

Was her apartment even reasonably tidy? She didn't have any food. Well, not the kind of food to entertain with and make dinner for a guest. Chilli-flavoured crisps and orange-flavoured chocolate might be her favourite dinner but she couldn't offer it to a guest. What on earth had she been thinking?

She was desperately hoping that she appeared outwardly calm. But her heartbeat was thudding against her chest at a rate of knots. Logan gestured to the waiter and settled their bill, picking up his bag and giving her a casual smile. 'Shall we finish this paperwork back at your place?'

It was a reasonable, rational question. He couldn't possibly imagine the way the blood was racing around her system and the breath was sticking in her lungs.

'Of course,' she said as coolly as possible, with a nod of her head as she stood up.

'How far away do you live?' he asked.

She tried to smile. 'Well, that depends entirely on traffic and the time of day.'

She weaved her way through the cobbled streets towards the water-taxi stop. 'I'm only two stops along. It only takes a few minutes.'

They were lucky. The water taxis on this side of the canal weren't quite so busy. They jumped on and back off within five minutes.

Her skin was prickling. Every little hair on her arms was standing on end even though the sun was splitting the sky. Now that Logan had had a chance to cool down he was back to his normal, unruffled self. She kind of wished he was still as flustered as he had been for a few moments earlier. It made him seem less infallible. A little more vulnerable—just like she felt.

But Logan had never been vulnerable. He'd always been rock solid. Even in grief.

He jumped out of the taxi before her and held out his hand for her as she stepped from the bobbing boat. She lifted her head and tried to walk with confidence. Although her apartment overlooked the Grand Canal the entrance of the traditional building was around the back. It had been hundreds of years since people had entered directly from the canal, and the original entrance had long since been plastered over.

She couldn't hide her smile. The architect in Logan could never be hidden. His eyes were roaming over the traditional building, his smile growing wider by the second. 'You stay in an old Venetian palace?'

The admiration and wonder in his voice was obvious. She'd always known Logan would approve of her choice. The fifteenth-century building facing the Grand Canal was one of the most photographed in the district. It had distinctive Venetian floral Gothic-style architecture. The façade was pink plaster facing with intricate white detailing around all the windows and balconies that overlooked the canal. The arches on the balconies were topped with delicate quatrefoil windows, resembling flowers with four petals.

She gave him a smile as she opened the entranceway. 'Just wait until you see the inside. We have our own high ceilings, beams, alcoves and frescoes. The whole place is full of original features.'

Logan was nodding, his eyes wide as they stepped inside. She'd always loved this about him. The way a glimpse of architectural details of a building could capture his attention instantly. He would become instantly enthralled, desperate to know more about the building and its history. Architecture had always been Logan's dream. But renovating ancient buildings? That was his calling. Always had been.

A bit like hers had been painting.

The memory swept through her like a gust of stormy weather.

Another part of life put into a box. When she'd first got together with Logan, their apartment had been littered with brushes, easels and oils. She had painted all the time, usually wearing nothing more than one of his shirts. She'd loved the feel of having him right next to her as she'd created, and if he hadn't been there, the scent of him—his aroma and aftershave—would usually linger on one of his shirts waiting to be washed. Thoughts of Logan had always fired her creative juices.

A warm feeling crept across her stomach. Logan had always loved finding her like that, his shirt loose around her body and her hair twisted on top of her head with an errant paint-brush holding it in place. He'd usually pulled it free, followed by the shirt, and the following hours had been lost in a rush of love.

But that light had flickered out and died along with the death of their daughter. For a long time she couldn't even bear to look at a paintbrush, let alone hold one.

Working for the heritage board had helped her heal. She didn't paint her own creations any more. But she did paint. Restoration work was painstaking. In every fresco she restored she tried to re-create the passion and drama that the original artist had felt when he'd envisaged the work.

There was still a little part of her that longed to feel like that again too.

There was a lift inside her building but Logan

was captivated by the grandiose staircase inside the entranceway. As it curved upwards there were archways hollowed out in the plaster in the walls. A long time ago each had been painted individually and had held sculptures. In between each hollowed archway was a large circular fresco embedded into the plaster on the walls.

Logan moved quickly up the stairs, stopping to admire each individual one. 'These are amazing,' he said, his hand hovering about them. Logan's professional expertise knew far better than to actually touch.

She followed him upwards. A warmth was spreading through her. She was proud of her home—and secretly pleased that the man she'd shared part of her life with loved it just as much as she did.

As they walked upwards she leaned a little closer and whispered, 'I might have restored some of these.'

His head shot around towards her. 'You did?'

She nodded as his eyes fixed on the walls again. His fingers were still hovering just above a fresco of Moses. 'You've made an amazing job of these.'

'Thank you,' she said simply, as they reached her floor and she pulled out her key and opened the apartment door.

He walked inside and looked around. Her living area was spacious and held a dining table and chairs and two wooden-footed red sofas. As with most Italian traditional apartments the floor was marble. A dark wooden bookcase adorned one wall, jam-packed with books.

But the most spectacular aspect of the apartment was the view. Lucia strode across the room and pulled open the black-and-gilt-edged glass doors. The warm air and noise from the Grand Canal below flooded in. It was like flicking a button and bringing the place to life. Next to the doors was a small wooden table, a chaise longue and an armchair. It was like having a real-live television. You could sit here all day and night and watch the world go by.

She knew his head must be spinning. This apartment was sumptuous. Well out of her price range. She stood shoulder to shoulder with him, watching the *vaporetti* and private boats motor past. On the other side of the canal stood another magnificent long-abandoned palace. Renaissance in style again, with Gothic-styled windows and ornate frescoes on the outside of the building.

He turned towards her and smiled. 'It's almost like your perfect view, isn't it?' There was an edge of curiosity in his voice. But he wasn't going to ask the question out loud. Logan was far too polite for that.

'Coffee?' she asked, as she walked towards the kitchen. It was right next door to the open living area and again had windows looking out on the canal. He nodded and walked in next to her, sitting down on one of the high stools looking over the canal. She switched on her coffee-machine and put in her favourite blend.

She leaned back against the countertop. 'I haven't always stayed here,' she said quietly. 'After I'd been in Venice for two years one of my colleagues retired from the heritage board. They subsidise our living arrangements because—as you know—Venice can be very expensive.' She held out her hands. 'I sort of inherited this place. I pay roughly the same as we did for our apartment in Florence.' She watched his eyebrows rise and couldn't stop the smile. 'It was like all my Saturdays at once.' She laughed as she watched the coffee brew and pointed across the waterway. 'Do you know, they actually asked me how I'd feel about staying here? It was all I could do not to snatch the key and just run.'

The warm feeling was spreading further. She rarely brought friends back to her apartment. This place was her sanctuary. From the moment she'd stepped inside it had always felt like that.

She'd thought having Logan here would be unbearable. She'd been so busy focusing on all the negatives she hadn't even considered the positives.

He was fascinated by the building's history and traditional architecture. He respected the heritage just as much as she did.

She poured the coffee into two mugs and set them on the table, watching the steam rising while she frothed some milk and added it to the mugs.

She gestured with her hand. 'Come and I'll show you where your room is.'

She hadn't even had time to prepare anything and she had to hope that nothing was out of place in her barely used guest suite. She led him down the corridor off the kitchen. It was the only place in her apartment that didn't have natural light.

He grabbed her elbow as they walked down the corridor. 'Are you sure this is okay?'

She turned to face him. He was much closer than she'd expected, his warm breath hitting her cheek. For a second she was frozen. This was as up close and personal as she'd been to Logan in years. The closeness took her breath away.

Even in the dim light of the corridor his green eyes made her struggle to think clearly. He was worried. He was worried about her. And glances like that brought back painful memories.

A tiny little part of her wished that Logan was looking at her in a different way. The way he used to, with passion and laughter in his eyes. She wanted to reach up and touch him. Touch the skin on his cheek, the shadowed outline of his jaw, and run her fingers through his dark hair. She wanted him to step forward just a few inches to see if their bodies still fitted together after all this time.

Her heart was racing and Logan blinked. He was staring at a spot on her neck where she was sure he could see the rapid beating of her pulse.

She took a deep breath and turned away, trying to blink back threatening tears. This was why everything about this was a bad idea.

She swung open a dark wooden door, flooding the corridor with light and stepping into a white and blue room. It was still traditional. A double bedroom with a window overlooking the canal, pale blue walls and fresh white bed linen. It wasn't quite as sumptuous as the other rooms in the house as it was rarely used.

She nodded her head. 'The bathroom is next door. Don't worry, we won't have to share. The box room was converted to an en suite. Would you like some time to settle in?'

He shook his head. 'Your coffee smells too good to let it go to waste. Let's finish the paperwork then we can decide where I'm taking you to dinner.' There was a glimmer in his eye. 'I don't expect you to cook for me—not if I want to live to tell the tale.'

He'd caught her unawares and she threw back her head and laughed. 'I offer you a room for the night and this is the thanks I get?'

He gave her a steady smile. 'Let's just wait until dinner.' She could almost hear his brain ticking over and her stomach gave a little leap.

What on earth did he have planned?

Logan washed up and changed his wrinkled shirt. Thank goodness he always had a spare in his bag.

He looked around the room. It was comfortable but sparse—it was clear this room didn't get much use. Didn't Lucia have friends to stay? She'd had a few girlfriends at university but he had no idea if they'd kept in touch.

He sighed and looked out of the window. It was ridiculous but he was having a hard time with this.

Lucia had a job she loved and a fabulous apartment in one of the most cosmopolitan cities in the world. He should be overjoyed for her. In his head, all he'd ever wanted was for her to be happy. In a twisted kind of way this was his ideal situation.

She was happy. She was settled. But there was no husband and kids on the scene to let the tiny leaves of jealousy unfurl. To let him know that she'd taken the final steps.

He couldn't quite work out why he was feeling so unsettled. All he knew was that there was something in her eyes. A guarded part. A hidden part. A little piece of her that didn't look quite…alive.

That was what bothered him. Lucia had a fabulous life. But was she really living?

He glanced around. While this room was sparsely furnished, the rest of the apartment was sumptuous. The reds and golds complemented the grandeur of the ancient palace. There were lots of similar buildings scattered across Venice. It seemed everyone who'd ever been slightly royal had built a palace in Venice. It was no wonder the heritage board wanted to keep someone in here.

He walked through to the main room. Lucia was sitting in a chair next to the open doors, the sights and sounds of the Grand Canal drifting up towards them. She'd changed into a purple jersey wrap-around dress, her dark chocolate-brown hair falling over her shoulders in waves. Her legs were curled up underneath her and she was reading a book.

Sitting on the table next to her was a glass of red wine. He smiled. 'Merlot or Chianti?'

Her head lifted in surprise. 'What do you think?'

He glanced out at the busy traffic on the Grand Canal. 'A warm summer evening? An aperitif before dinner?' He put his finger on his chin. 'I'm trying to think what you've planned for dinner—will it be meat or pasta?'

She used to be so fussy. He could imagine there were only certain local restaurants that she'd visit.

She held up her glass towards him. 'Maybe it will be both?'

She was teasing. He shook his head and pointed

to the glass. 'It must be Merlot. It's too warm an evening for steak. You're planning for pasta.'

Something flickered across her face. She didn't like it that after twelve years he could still read her. She gestured towards the dining table where the bottle of wine and another glass sat. 'Find out for yourself.'

Logan walked over and filled his glass, resisting the temptation to smile. 'Where do you think we're eating tonight?'

She raised her eyebrows. 'What makes you think we'll be eating anywhere? Haven't you heard—it's the busiest night of the year in Venice?'

He sat down on the chaise longue next to her chair. 'But I might know an out-of-the-way place that the tourist hordes don't know about—like Erona's in Florence.'

There was a flash of something behind her eyes and she stood up quickly. He'd upset her.

She didn't want direct reminders of their time in Florence. 'You're not from here. How would you know where to eat?'

'Let's just say that your boss, Alessio, gave me a few hints.'

She slid her feet into a pair of red-soled black patent stilettos with impossibly high heels.

'Wherever we're going, I hope they have flat surfaces,' he muttered. Alessio had told him to get to the restaurant—just not what the streets around it were like.

'Let's go, Logan. Our viewing is early tomorrow morning. I want to get an early night.'

The words sent a flurry of sparks across his brain. An early night. With Lucia Moretti. It was enough to send his whole body into overdrive.

His eyes focused on her behind as she crossed the room ahead of him in her impossibly high heels. Her dress clung to every curve.

He swallowed. This was going to be a long, uncomfortable night.

Venice was virtually silent at this time in the morning. The private motor boat glided through the water towards the Venetian island of Giudecca.

Logan was curious. 'I thought all the artefacts

of historical value would have been comman-
deered by the Italian Heritage Board?'

Lucia gave a sigh. 'In theory, they can. But
part of this island is private—has been since
before Renaissance times. It's owned by the
Brunelli family. They built the church here
and commissioned the artist, Burano, to paint
the fresco. Technically, we're just their guests.
We're allowed access to the fresco on request.
You'll understand why when you see it—it's a
little unusual.'

The boat came to a halt at the dock and they
disembarked onto the wooden structure. A white
stone path led them directly to the church, where
a dark-suited man was waiting for them. Logan
recognised him immediately—Dario Brunelli
was frequently nicknamed Italian's most eligi-
ble bachelor. *He knew Lucia?*

'Lucia,' he said swiftly, bending to kiss her on
both cheeks, 'it's good to see you again. How
have you been?'

His familiarity with Lucia grated instantly.
Her reaction was even worse—she seemed relaxed in his company. 'I'm good, thank you.'

She turned towards Logan. 'Dario, this is Logan Cascini, a specialist restoration architect from Florence. He's working with me on the project in Tuscany.'

It was completely true. But it made it sound as if they'd only just met. As if there was no shared history between them at all.

For a second he held his breath, wondering if Dario was having the same thoughts that he'd had this morning when he'd first seen Lucia. Her cream fitted business suit and pale pink shirt hugged her curves. The knee-length skirt exposed her slim legs. And her dark hair and eyes complemented the package perfectly. Lucia looked good enough to eat.

Dario nodded towards Logan but it was clear his focus was on Lucia. 'So, do you think you've found another of Burano's frescoes?'

Lucia's smile was broad. 'I think there is a distinct possibility. With your permission, I'm going to take some high-resolution digital shots to compare the brushstrokes.'

Dario was nodding enthusiastically. 'In Tuscany? I wonder how in the world Burano ended up working there? Wouldn't it be wonderful if it was another of his works?'

A Renaissance art lover. The passion and enthusiasm in his eyes was for the art, not for Lucia. Not for his woman.

Where had that come from?

Cold air prickled his skin and he shifted on his feet. Lucia hadn't been his woman for twelve years—she hadn't wanted to be.

And he'd had to live with that. He'd had to support the fact she wasn't able to continue their relationship and allow her the space she'd needed to heal. No matter how much it had ripped his heart in two.

No one else had ever come close to the love he'd felt for Lucia. How could they? She'd been the mother of his child. And even though that was something she wanted to forget, her place in his heart had been well and truly cemented there.

But even he hadn't realised how much.

'Forgive me.' Dario nodded. 'I have to go. I have business to attend to. Please, take all the time you need.'

Lucia gave a gracious nod of her head as Dario walked swiftly down the path towards the waiting motorboat.

She turned and pressed her hand against the heavy wooden door of the church and smiled at Logan. There was a gleam of something in her eye. He only hoped it was for the contents of the church and not for the retreating back of Dario. The spike of jealousy had been unexpected—a feeling he hadn't dealt with in years.

'Ready?' she asked.

He nodded and she pushed the door and it groaned and creaked loudly on its hinges as it swung back. The church wasn't lit.

The only light that streamed in came through six muted stained-glass windows above the altar.

It took a few seconds for his eyes to adjust to the dim light. He caught his breath.

The fresco on the wall was magnificent and stretched from one end of the church to the other. His feet moved automatically towards it.

Over his years in Italy he'd seen many frescoes—but none quite like this. It was completely and utterly unique, almost like a timeline through the first book of the bible.

She rested her hand on his arm. 'I've never seen anything like it before, and I'm quite sure I'll never see anything like it again.' He could hear the amusement in her voice at his reaction. 'It's a little different from the Madonna and Child, isn't it?'

He shook his head as he took in more and more of the fresco. He recognised the characters—at least, he thought he did. Adam and Eve, Noah, Moses, Jacob and his sons. But the thing that made these characters unique was the fact they were all completely naked.

He spun to face her. 'What on earth…?'

She laughed. 'I know. It's why the Italian Heritage Board hasn't bothered to make demands on the family. The Catholic Church would be outraged by these scenes.'

Logan moved forward. He just couldn't stop smiling. He was trying to think rationally. 'Adam and Eve—you might expect them to be naked. But the rest…' He kept looking at the scenes. 'It's amazing. I mean, apart from their nakedness the depictions are accurate. Eve with the apple, Moses leading the Israelites through the Red Sea, Noah on the ark, and Jacob with his twelve sons.' He let out a laugh. 'Joseph is even holding his multi-coloured coat instead of wearing it.'

She shrugged her shoulders. 'Naked bodies were pretty much the fashion during Renaissance times.' Her brow creased slightly. 'But usually they had something—anything—draped around about them. These ones are totally original.'

Logan stepped back a little. 'But there's something else, isn't there? I can't quite put my finger on it.' He paused, staring hard at the scenes, looking between one and another.

She nodded, with an amused expression on her face. 'Give it time, Logan. You'll get it.'

She was teasing him. It was almost like throwing down a challenge. So he took a few minutes, concentrating hard until, finally, the penny dropped.

He turned to her in amazement. 'It's the faces, isn't it?' He stepped right up to the fresco, staring first at the face of Adam then at the face of Moses, then Noah. 'It's the same face.' His eyes scanned one way, then the other. 'It's the same man and woman in every scene.'

Lucia was laughing. 'You're right. The family don't have any official records about who commissioned the fresco. The name of Burano has just been passed down through the family. That's why we'll have to do a comparison. And we're not quite sure why it's the same faces in all the scenes. I've spoken to the family about it at length. We think there's something a little narcissistic in it. We think that when the original Brunellis commissioned the artist they asked for the faces to be made in their image.'

Logan let out a burst of laughter. 'You mean, even all those years ago we had fame-hungry people?' He shook his head. 'Wow, just wow.'

He took another few seconds and stopped in front of the young Joseph holding the coat. 'I still can't believe they wouldn't let Joseph wear his multi-coloured coat.'

She bent down in the front of the fresco. In

the dim light he could see her dark eyes were still gleaming. 'Yes, but look at the folds in the cloak. What do you see?'

He looked closer. 'Of course. They look exactly like the folds in the Madonna's dress in the fresco in Tuscany. That's what you noticed.'

There wasn't a sound in the dark church. They were entirely alone, crouching on the floor. The lack of artificial light was almost like a safety blanket around them.

His face was only inches from hers. Their gazes meshed. It was a moment. An instant. For just that second she had the same passion and wonder in her eyes that she'd had twelve years ago. Twelve years ago when they'd thought they could conquer the world.

He'd been trying so hard to hold his tongue, trying to keep a handle on how he felt about everything, but the memories of Lucia were just overtaking him. The spark of jealousy, the protectiveness, the connection between them. He was like a pressure cooker just waiting to go off.

Her pupils were dilating in front of him, the blackness overtaking the chocolate brown of her eyes. He was pretty certain his were doing exactly the same.

All of a sudden he couldn't stop himself. He leaned forward, just a few inches, and caught the back of her head in his hand, tangling his fingers through her hair as he pulled her towards him.

And then he stopped thinking entirely...

She was instantly transported back twelve years. The familiarity was astounding.

No one had kissed her like this in twelve years.

No kiss had felt so right.

No kiss had felt so perfect.

Her body moved on automatic pilot, ignoring all the little neurons that were firing in her brain. Ignoring every single rational thought that might be there.

She could only act on instinct. Her hands slid through his thick, dark hair, her fingers tugging and pulling at his head. She could taste him. She could smell him.

Everything about him was familiar. His scent was winding its way around her like a coiling snake. Her hands moved, sliding across his muscled shoulders and arms and down the planes of his chest.

His lips never left hers. Their teeth clashed, his tongue tangling with hers. Crouching on a floor wasn't comfortable for kissing. Logan sensed that and pulled her up against him, his strong legs lifting them both upwards, keeping their bodies in contact the whole time.

She could feel his heart thudding against her chest. Feel her breath catching in her throat.

It was so easy to be swept away. It was so easy to forget about everything else. His fingertips brushed across the front of her breasts as she sucked in a sharp breath, then rounded her hips and stopped firmly on her behind, pulling her even closer to him.

There was no mistaking his reaction to her. There was no mistaking he was every bit as caught up in this as she was.

So when he stopped kissing her she was shocked.

He pulled his lips back from hers and rested his forehead against hers, breathing heavily. His body was still interlocked with hers. It seemed he had no intention of moving.

Her hands, resting against his chest, clenched.

Embarrassment swamped her. She wanted to step back but couldn't.

What on earth was he thinking?

Then, to her surprise, he let out a deep laugh. It wasn't a mocking laugh. It wasn't derogatory. It was more one of astonishment.

In the dark church his voice was husky. 'So that's what I've been missing.' He took a deep breath. 'I sometimes wondered if my mind was playing tricks on me. If I'd imagined how good it was.'

He was echoing her thoughts. She'd felt exactly the same way. Any time she'd allowed memories of Logan to sneak into her brain, she'd always thought it couldn't possibly have been as good as she remembered it. Everything before Ariella Rose, that was.

The portcullis that was always stiffly in place

was shaken a little. The thick gate had risen just a tiny bit, leaving the thinnest gap underneath. The black cloud of self-protection that usually cloaked her was thinning in patches.

Their foreheads were still touching. She could feel his warm breath on her cheeks. 'It wasn't all that bad, was it?' she whispered.

His fingers stroked through her soft hair. 'Some parts were really good,' he breathed quietly.

She stayed where she was—for a few more seconds.

This was only a moment of madness. A tiny little step back in time.

It wasn't real. None of this was real.

Real life meant that now she lived and worked in Venice and Logan lived and worked in Florence.

The meeting at Tuscany was merely a blip. The next few weeks of working together would only be a continuation of that blip. She could almost feel the protective coating going around her heart. She had to be careful. She had to be sensible.

She lifted her head back from his, trying to ignore the warm feeling of his beating heart beneath her palm.

It was time to put all the safeguards back in place.

She gave him a rueful smile and stepped back, freeing herself from his grasp.

The movement jolted Logan. He straightened his back, watching her carefully. It was almost as if he knew what was coming next.

'We don't really have time to reminisce, Logan. I have work to do. You have work to do. The sooner we can verify the artist of the fresco, the sooner we can both move towards our goals.'

What were her goals? She'd always been clear about them in the past, but right now they were looking pretty muddy.

Silence hung in the air between them. It almost shimmered in the slowly brightening daylight.

She could almost hear him processing what she'd said.

He chose his words carefully as he stepped forward and gently touched her cheek. 'You're right, Lucia. It's best we leave things as they are.' He nodded his head. 'We both need to focus on work.'

Something squeezed in her chest. For a few seconds she felt as if she couldn't breathe.

Part of her wished he'd said no. Part of her wished he'd pull her back into his arms and kiss her all over again. Acknowledge this thing that shimmered in the air between them and refuse to walk away from it.

But that was all a fairy tale. This was real life. She could tell from the slight waver in his voice that he was saying what he thought he should. This was just as hard for him as it was for her.

If this was anyone else she might think they were toying with her. But Logan just wasn't capable of that kind of thing. Not after what they'd shared.

This was for the best. It didn't matter that little parts of her brain were screaming at her. Every female hormone she'd ever possessed was currently marching in a charge towards all parts of her body.

She blinked back the tears that were hovering behind her eyes. His fingers felt like butterfly wings on her skin. It was all she could do not to tilt her head towards his hand.

She bent down and picked up her papers, which were strewn on the floor, trying not to acknowledge her trembling hands.

His feet took a step backwards. She could sense him bending over her, probably reaching towards her, then he took a few further steps back. It was almost as if he forcing himself into a position of retreat.

She straightened up and fixed a false smile on her face. 'Let's get to work, Logan. Can you see if we can find some light?' She pulled her camera from her bag. 'The sooner we get these pictures, the sooner we can move forward.'

She tried not to wince at her choice of words.

But Logan's expression was resolute. Guarded. She had no idea what was going on behind those green eyes.

He gave a brief nod. 'Of course.' And walked back towards the door to let in some light.

She turned back to the fresco.

Work. The only thing that was currently keeping her sane.

CHAPTER SIX

WORK WAS THE easy part. It didn't take any time at all for Lucia to take the photos and to take the boat trip back to her office. The rest of Venice had woken up now, with the city becoming loud and colourful as their boat glided back through the water.

The Italian Heritage Board building was every bit as exuberant as Logan had expected it to be. The architecture was a welcome distraction, with some of the really exclusive Renaissance pieces of art housed in the building.

Lucia had uploaded the pictures to her computer and was running a comparison computer program that would take a few hours.

All they could do was wait.

And waiting was something Logan Cascini had never been good at.

After that kiss he was finding it difficult to

keep his cool, collected manner in place. One touch of Lucia's lips had been enough to ignite all the sparks in his brain and frustration had been building ever since.

He'd had enough. Not of Lucia. He'd had enough of them being in the same room together and not talking about the big elephant between them. Ariella Rose.

It was twelve years on. It was time. Even if Lucia still felt that it wasn't.

There was no way he was getting on that plane back to Tuscany without tackling the subject. No way at all.

But how?

She had barriers erected so tightly around her she might as well have been wearing a space-suit. The kiss had been one thing. She'd probably already written it off as a blip.

But Logan couldn't do that. He wanted more. Much more.

No wonder every other relationship he'd had had fizzled out. No wonder he'd never wanted to commit to someone else.

This was nothing to do with losing his daughter. This wasn't about the fear of another pregnancy or another child.

It was much more primal than that. It was about the fear of never finding someone he had the same chemistry with, the same connection with, as he had with Lucia.

Life was hard. Life was tough. But twelve years of drifting had given him new determination.

Seeing Lucia for the first time again had been like a lightning bolt. Kissing her again...well, that had been so much more.

It was time to face things head-on.

He turned from the view of Venice to face her. She was sitting behind her desk, twiddling her long dark hair around one finger.

He reached forward and grabbed her other hand, pulling her to her feet. 'Let's go.'

She looked shocked. 'Let's go where?'

He held out his other hand. 'Out there. Let's see Venice.' He pointed to the screen. 'You already said the computer program would take a few hours. Let's spend them wisely.' He grinned at her. 'Today I am a tourist. Today I want you to show me Venice.'

A hint of a smile appeared on her face. She waved towards the window. 'But it will be crazy out there. There's another concert tonight. We'll have all of last night's gig-goers and all of tonight's too.'

He raised his eyebrows. 'What, we can't handle a few tourists?'

She shook her head and let out a little laugh. 'Now I know you're definitely crazy.' She picked up her handbag and swung it over her shoulder. 'You're right, the program will take another few hours, and as long as we start with ice cream I'm in.'

He held out his hand towards her.

She hesitated. She wavered. He could see it in every inch of her body. She finally let out the breath she'd been holding and put her hand in his.

'Let's go.'

It was hotter than hot. Her jacket was hanging over the top of her shoulder bag to try and deter any pickpockets and her shirt was in danger of sticking to her back.

The queue for ice cream was snaking its way out the door of her favourite gelateria. She tugged Logan towards the end of the queue. His hand was still in hers. It felt odd, but she hadn't quite managed to pull her hand free of his.

The walk through the twisting cobbled streets had been like a step back in time. She'd noticed the women's admiring glances. Logan was every woman's Italian dream—dark-haired, broad shouldered, well dressed and devilishly handsome. His unexpected bright green eyes added a little twist.

And he was free with his natural charm. He nodded and smiled at the numerous pairs of acknowledging eyes. A tiny swell of pride surged in her chest. Memories flickered in her brain. People thought they were a couple. People thought that Logan was hers.

He turned to face her as the queue slowly moved forward. 'What kind of ice cream do you want? I take it you've sampled them all?'

She gave a little smile. 'All in the name of research. Dark chocolate and *limon* are my two favourites from here.'

He nodded at her choices. 'In that case we'll get one of each. Why not try everything you like?' He was smiling as he said the words, and the woman in front turned around with a gleam in her eyes.

Lucia shifted on her feet. She didn't want to allow the tiny seeds in her brain to flower and grow.

Logan reached the front of the queue, ordering their ice creams and only releasing her hand when he reached to pay for them. They walked out into the building heat and he held both hands out towards her. 'What'll it be? The dark, tantalising chocolate or the sweet, zesty lemon?'

He was teasing her. But the surprising thing was, she kind of liked it.

She held her hand out for the chocolate. 'I'll start with dark and delicious.' Her fingers brushed against his. 'But don't count on getting to finish the lemon yourself,' she said smartly as she walked past.

Within seconds he was walking shoulder to

shoulder with her. 'Where do you want to play tourist, then?' she asked. 'I can't imagine that you want to visit Piazza San Marco, St Mark's Basilica or the Clock Tower.'

He shook his head. 'Too busy, and anyway I much prefer Piazza San Marco at night. Much more romantic,' he added.

She ignored the comment.

He pointed over in the distance. 'What I'd really like to do is catch a *vaporetto* to San Giorgio Maggiore and go up the campanile. It's still early. There will hardly be any crowds.'

She gave him a sideways glance as she veered towards the nearest *vaporetto* stop. 'Hmm, so you're still a tourist at heart, then?'

He shrugged. 'It's been a few years since I've been in Venice. But I'm an Italian, I still know where to go to get the best view of the city.' He held out his ice cream towards her. 'Swap?'

She nodded. The dark chocolate was starting to taste a little bitter. She took a nibble of the lemon and sweet, tangy zest nearly made her taste buds explode. But her brain didn't have time to focus on that because Logan had slung his arm around her shoulders and was walking easily next to her as if they did it every day.

And it *did* feel like they did it every day. She fitted under his arm. Always had—always would.

He chatted as they made their way along to the *vaparetto* stop, joining the small number of waiting people and climbing on board as soon as it arrived. Most of the rest of the passengers were heading to Murano—the island famous for its glassware. He glanced at her as the boat stopped. 'Did you want to get off here?'

She shook her head. 'I love Murano glass— I have the most gorgeous red and gold vase in my apartment—but I don't like the hordes of tourists, or what they make for them. If I see one more orange fish in a clear square cube I'll scream.'

She was standing near the front of the boat and he laughed and pulled her down next to him as the next load of passengers climbed on board. 'You old Venice snob.'

'Oh, come on, you were exactly the same way

in Florence. You hated the millions of ornaments of the cathedral and baptistery.'

He lifted his ice cream towards her. 'Guilty as charged.' Then he glanced at the activity on the Grand Canal. 'But sometimes it's nice to play tourist.'

They sat in silence for a few minutes as the boat glided along the canal. It was busy this morning, making the ride a little bumpy, and she inched closer and closer to him. His arm stayed loosely on her shoulders as they reached the stop for San Giorgio. Ice creams finished, they wiped their hands on the napkins provided and climbed out of the boat.

It was getting hotter but most of the tourists hadn't reached the island yet and the queue for the lift to the top of the campanile meant they only had a ten-minute wait.

Logan shook his head as they approached. 'This is one of the architectural glories of Venice. Palladio is one of my favourite architects. Look at it, the gleaming white Istrian marble façade and lithe brick and bell tower—why, it almost seems to float in the middle of the

Bacino San Marco, supported on its own tiny island. It's only a few hundred yards off St Mark's Square but most people just take a photo on the way past. They have no idea it's decorated with works by Tintoretto, Carpaccio and Jacopo Bassano. This is the one place in Venice I just wouldn't want to miss.'

Lucia smiled at him. The passion and enthusiasm in his voice was so good to hear. She could see heads turning at his voice, obviously relieved they'd chosen this venue to visit.

The lift opened to take them up the sixty-metre-high bell tower and a few minutes later they stepped out on to the observation deck. Logan held out his arms and spun around. 'And this is why I love this place. Hardly a queue to get in, only a couple of euros and no crowding up here. The view is perfect.' He pointed across the water towards the campanile San Marco. 'While our brother over there has long lines, a higher price tag, is crowded and doesn't have the same panoramic views.'

Lucia grinned. 'But you can get a full-on post-card shot of the Piazza San Marco just across the water.' She pulled out her phone and held it in front of her, snapping a quick photo.

'Hold it.' Logan pulled out his own phone, but put his hands on her shoulders and turned her, so instead of having a background shot of Piazza San Marco he had a full shot of the Grand Canal. 'Smile,' he said as he held up his phone. 'You know, on a clear day you can see right across the Adriatic Sea and all the way to the Alps.'

The smile was still on her face and she didn't have much time to think about the fact that Logan would now have a picture of her on his phone. As soon as he'd snapped the shot he walked over and leaned his elbows on the balcony, looking out at the panoramic view. 'This is what Venice should be about,' he said quietly.

She spun around and put her elbows next to his. There were a few other people wandering around on the observation deck, but it was nowhere near as busy here as it was on the other side of the water. St Mark's Square was already packed. It seemed most of the people who'd attended the concert hadn't had much sleep.

She could hardly blame them. Anyone who was lucky enough to visit Venice—even for a few hours—usually tried to squeeze in as many of the sights as they possibly could.

Something flickered through her brain. With one concert last night and another tonight there would be a whole host of new people in and out of the city today. 'You won't be able to get a flight home today either, will you?'

A gentle breeze blew across her skin. She wasn't quite sure how she felt about this. Having Logan stay over one night had seemed like an unavoidable hiccup. Having him stay for two nights was something else entirely.

He didn't answer for a few seconds, fixing his eyes instead on the hustle and bustle of the masses of people on the other side of the canal. 'I'm sorry, Lucia.' He ran his fingers through his hair. 'I had no idea about any of this. I didn't mean to put you in a difficult position.'

He looked a little uncomfortable but not entirely unhappy. She'd hardly slept a wink last night. How could she, knowing that the person she used to love with her whole heart had been lying naked next door?

Logan had always slept naked, hating anything on his skin once he was in bed. The only thing he'd ever wanted next to his skin had been her.

She was trying so hard to seem cool, to seem professional. The atmosphere between them today had been lighter, less pressured.

Exactly the opposite from what it should have been after that kiss.

But that kiss had ignited the good memories in her brain. Before that, everything about Logan had been a build-up of frustration and a reminder of grief.

It was almost as if that kiss had brought alive the side of her brain she'd shut off. She just didn't know what to do with it.

'It's fine, Logan,' she said quickly, as she held out her hand towards the busy St Mark's Square. 'The hotels will be every bit as busy again today. Don't worry.'

His head turned towards her and he lifted his hand, running one finger down her arm towards her hand. 'But I do worry, Lucia. I'll always worry about you.' His voice was low, husky and it sent a little tremble up her spine.

She couldn't turn to face him, just kept looking out at the people of Venice as her skin tingled and his hand slid over hers, slowly interlocking their fingers.

Her breath caught in her chest. Just when she'd thought she was safe around Logan. Just when she'd thought she could relax, he did something like this.

Something that made her catch her breath and nibble her bottom lip.

It was the closeness that made her feel vulnerable. Made her feel as if she was on the verge of opening herself up to a whole host of hurt. She'd spent so long protecting herself, hiding herself away.

Logan was a whole part of her life that she'd chosen to close the door on. But having him standing next to her, his breath warming her cheek and his hand interlocked with hers, was like dangling her over a precipice she wasn't ready for.

And it was as if he could sense it. He didn't go any further. Didn't make any other move. Didn't bring up the biggest subject in the world.

Logan was carefully skirting around the edges of her life. But he wouldn't stay there for ever.

'How do you enjoy living and working in Venice?'

She swallowed, trying to push all other thoughts away. 'I love Venice. But it's not the city that captures my soul. I still miss Florence.'

The words took her by surprise. She'd always felt like that. She'd just never said it out loud.

He was facing her again and she could feel his eyes watching her carefully. She wondered if he'd pick her up on what she'd just said. But he didn't. He let it go, keeping things in safe territory. 'How do the restorations work?'

She lifted her other hand and pulled her hair off her neck. It was getting even hotter. 'I've done at least one every year I've worked for the heritage board. Always on frescoes. If they decide the fresco in Tuscany is genuine and is to be restored, then that will be my job.'

She knew why he was asking. He would be

in Tuscany for the next few months and he was trying to think ahead. If a few days were difficult, how would they manage to work in the same environment for a few months?

At least, she thought that's what would be on his mind.

It couldn't be the kiss. It *wouldn't* be the kiss. Not when there was so much more to think about.

'How do you feel about coming down to Tuscany?'

It was work. Of course it was work. She didn't know whether to feel disappointment or relief. The touching and handholding was nothing. It was just Logan back to his usual charming self, trying to make everyone around him feel good.

She stared at the packed street across from her and smiled. 'While I love Venice, and I love my apartment, the summer months are extremely busy. Tuscany seems a lot more peaceful than here. It might be nice to have some clean fresh air and some quiet to be able to concentrate on the restoration work.' She turned her body towards him, finally relaxed enough to give him a smile. 'I think I'll like it.'

But Logan wasn't staring at her the way she'd thought. He'd moved his thumb underneath their interlocked fingers and was gently making circles on the underside of her palm, This was what he'd used to do when he was deep in thought... when he was contemplating something carefully. His eyes were lowered and his voice quiet. 'How would you feel...?'

She inched a little closer to hear him.

He tried again. 'How would you feel if I asked you to stay with me when you came back to Tuscany, instead of in the main *palazzo* with Louise?'

Now he did look up. But he didn't have the quiet assuredness that usually always possessed him. Now he looked wary.

The words were very unexpected. She'd just gone back into that 'safe' zone, the one where no one could touch her and no one could threaten her. His words catapulted her straight back out.

The voices in the background blended together into one constant murmur as the rapid beating of her heart thudded in her eardrums. His thumb hadn't stopped moving in those little circles. It was almost as if he'd been trying to prepare her, to soothe her, before he'd asked the question.

Her brain felt jumbled. She didn't quite know what to say. 'I don't think...I don't think that would work,' was all she could fumble out.

His fingers tensed around hers. 'Why? Why wouldn't it work? You're my oldest friend. Twelve years have passed, Lucia, and you and I are still trapped there. Why aren't you married to someone else with a houseful of kids? Why aren't I?'

Now it was too much. That little question had turned into a whole lot more. She was standing overlooking this beautiful city, people all around her, and yet she felt hideously exposed. If she could transport herself, right now, back into her bed and under her covers, that's exactly what she'd do.

'I don't want to be married,' she blurted out, causing a few heads to turn in their direction. Instantly, she understood what she'd done. People were casting their eyes down in sympathy, as if Logan had just proposed and it had gone horribly wrong.

She shook her head. 'I'm happy with my work. I'm happy with my life.'

He put his hand behind her waist and pulled her towards him. His voice was quiet but there was an edge of frustration that only she could hear. Only she could understand.

'Look at me, Lucia. Look at me and tell me that you've tried to have other relationships. Tell me that you've met some suitably nice, handsome men—just like I've met some beautiful and good women—but something just hasn't been right. It hasn't felt the way it used to feel—the way it *should* feel. You could never go on and take the next step because you knew, deep down, that you'd ultimately hurt this good and loving person. You'd never quite love them the way that they loved you.'

It was almost as if he'd stepped inside her brain and was reading her mind and all her past memories. All her hidden regrets. She could see them all reflected on his face. He knew this, because he'd been living this life too.

That kiss had catapulted him into another space. Given him a painful reminder of what he wanted to capture again. Just like it had her.

She put her hand up to her chest, which was hurting, tight.

She was still shaking her head, aware of the anxious glances around them. 'I don't know, Logan. I just don't know.' She looked up and met his gaze. He looked hurt. He looked confused and something twisted inside her. It had been a long time since she and Logan had been like this.

Last time around she'd felt numb. She'd been unable to cope with her own grief so she certainly hadn't coped with his. But now he looked just as exposed as she felt.

His hair was mussed from where he'd run his fingers through it. The wind was rippling his shirt around his shoulders and chest. She almost hated the fact he could relate to how her life had turned out. To how every relationship she'd had since him had turned out.

But she hated even more that he'd mirrored her life with his own. She'd told herself that she'd always hoped Logan would move on, meet a girl, fall in love and have a family of his own.

Seeing him in Tuscany a few days ago and feeling that flicker of excitement when he'd told her he was unattached had revealed a side to her she didn't like.

He was fixed on her with those green eyes. They were burning a hole into her. To the rest of the world they would be the picture-perfect couple with the backdrop of Venice behind them. No one else would know the way their insides had been ripped out and left for the vultures.

Her heart squeezed. She was bad. She was selfish. Part of her did wish Logan had a happy life but then again part of her always wanted him to belong to her. But at what price?

He hadn't moved. One hand was still wrapped around her waist, pressing her body against his, the other interlocking their fingers. She could break free if she wanted to. But after all these years she just didn't know how.

He blinked. 'I won't pressure you any more. I won't bring it up again. Just promise me you'll give it some thought. You can tell me before I return to Tuscany tomorrow.'

She gave the briefest nod and it coincided with a swell of relief from her chest as he stepped back, breaking their contact. In their exposed position on the observation deck a gust of wind swept between them. It startled her, sweeping away the feeling of warmth from Logan's body next to hers.

The expression in Logan's eyes changed. Gone was the tiny smudge of vulnerability that she'd seen before. It had been replaced by the determined, focused look she knew so well.

'Are we done with photos?' he asked, just a little brusquely.

She nodded as she pushed her phone back in her bag. He took her hand again, firmly this time, no gentle touch, as if he was determined not to let her escape. They walked back to the lift. 'Tonight I'm going to pick the venue for dinner.'

It was clear there was no point arguing. She gave a brief nod as the doors slid closed in front of them.

The stiff atmosphere remained for the next thirty minutes. His hand grasped hers rigidly as they boarded the *vaporetto* and made the short journey back to Piazza San Marco.

It was even more crowded but Logan seemed to have got his bearings in the city and led her through some of the backstreets. Her phone rang just as they were about to cross one of Venice's bridges.

She pulled it from her bag. 'It's work,' she said. 'I need to take it.'

'No problem. I'll have a look in some of the shops around here.'

As her boss spoke rapidly in her ear she lost sight of Logan's broad shoulders in the crowds. It was twenty minutes before the conversation was over and Logan appeared at her side holding a large loop-handled bag with a designer logo on the side. He held it out towards her.

'What is it?'

'Yours. For tonight.'

She was more than a little surprised. She opened the bag and saw a flash of red but he shook his head.

'Leave it. You can try it on when we get back to the apartment.'

In some ways she should feel flattered. Logan had always had exquisite taste. He'd bought her clothes in the past and she'd loved every single item. But they weren't a couple any more—they weren't lovers and she wasn't sure this felt entirely appropriate.

'Why on earth would you buy me something?'

He shrugged his shoulders. 'It's a thank-you gift,' he said casually. 'A thank you for letting me stay at your apartment when I obviously should have planned better.' He made it sound so matter-of-fact, so easy and rational. But the contents of the bag didn't seem impartial.

Red was her favourite colour. And although she hadn't had a chance to examine the dress she was sure it would fit perfectly and be a flattering style. It was all part of Logan's gift.

'What was your call?' He wasn't giving her time to think about this too much. Probably in case she started to object.

She gave a little smile. 'The electronic comparison of brushstrokes indicates the fresco is indeed by Burano. The paint sampling won't be completed until early next week.'

'When?'

'Probably Monday. Technology is a wonderful thing these days. They will be able to give me an exact match of the product and colours that Burano used in his fresco for the restoration work.'

They started to walk across the bridge now, stopping in the middle just as a gondola with some tourists on board passed underneath. 'And how long do you think the restoration work will take?'

She put her elbows on the bridge next to him. The sun was beating down now, rising high in the sky above them. She gave a nervous laugh. 'That's the one thing that doesn't happen quickly. Probably around a few months.'

'And it will be definitely you who does the work?'

Was it possible he didn't want her to be working next to him, no matter what he'd been saying? Maybe Logan was only looking for a quiet life. Maybe he was only trying to keep her on-side to make sure his project didn't miss his deadline?

But he didn't look unhappy. He still had that determined gleam in his eye. He pointed to a baker's shop on the other side of the bridge. 'Why don't we grab some food and head back to the apartment? It's going to be too hot for sightseeing this afternoon and we both have work we can probably do before dinner tonight.'

She gave a nod of her head. It made sense— even if the thought of sharing her apartment space with Logan all afternoon made it feel as if the walls would close in around her.

'Where are we going later?' she asked, as they walked over the other side of the bridge.

He tapped the side of his nose. 'Leave that to me.'

CHAPTER SEVEN

IT WAS RIDICULOUS and he knew it. Why did he feel as if so much rested on one night?

He'd planned everything to perfection, pulling strings wherever he could. What he wanted most was for Lucia to be relaxed around him, maybe just enough to let her guard down and let him in.

It sounded cold, it sounded calculating. It was anything but.

He needed her to open up to him, to talk to him. It's what they both needed in order to move on with their lives.

It didn't matter that he had hopes for the direction in which they moved. He had to push those aside right now. He wanted her to talk. He couldn't see any further forward than that.

'Are you ready?'

He'd been pacing in the main room for the

last half hour, watching the sun beginning to lower in the sky, bathing Venice in a beautiful orange glow.

'I'm ready.' Her voice sounded a little shaky and he spun around.

She looked a picture. The red dress was exactly as he'd envisaged it, hugging her curves in all the right places. He'd known as soon as he'd seen it that it was perfect for her. A red jersey underlay with red crochet lace on top, it reached her knees and only gave the tiniest hint of skin underneath. Lucia had never liked anything too revealing.

She was wearing her black patent impossibly high heels with red soles and clutching a sequin bag in her hand. But something wasn't quite right.

She flicked her long hair on her shoulders and meshed her fingers together. Lucia was wound tighter than a spring.

He walked over and handed her a glass of red wine. 'Let's sit down for five minutes. We have time.'

He gestured towards the chaise longue.

She waited a few seconds. Her nerves seemed to emanate from her, and even the hand holding the glass had an almost imperceptible shake. After a few moments she sucked in a deep breath and walked across the room.

'Thank you for the dress. It's perfect,' she said simply, as she sat down and crossed her legs.

'I knew it would suit you,' he said calmly. 'You look stunning.' It was true and he was quite sure that every man in Venice who saw her would agree during the course of the evening.

She took a sip of her wine. 'Are you going to tell me where we are going for dinner?'

He smiled. 'We're in Venice. We're going to Rubins overlooking Piazza San Marco. Where else would we go?'

A hint of a smile appeared on her face as she relaxed back and took another sip of wine. 'How on earth did you manage that? You couldn't find a hotel room, but you managed to get into the most exclusive restaurant in Venice?'

He wrinkled his nose. 'Let's just say I might have helped them at some point with an architectural matter. Unfortunately, they don't have beds for the night—so dinner it is.'

He actually couldn't believe his luck. The restaurant overlooking Piazza San Marco and based in the Procuratie Nuove had had issues a few years ago when some of the stonework around the elaborate archways had started to crumble. Logan had been able to help them find the same stone, from the original source, to allow complete restoration. It hadn't been an easy task. And right now he would take any advantage he could get.

They sat for a few minutes longer, watching the world go by on the Grand Canal, as she finished her wine.

He stood up and held out his hand towards her. 'Are we ready?'

She nodded and slid her hand into his. The momentum of pulling her up made them almost bump noses and she laughed and put her hands on his chest. 'Where did this dark suit come from? You surely didn't have this in your bag?'

He shook his head. 'I picked it up an hour ago

when you were getting ready. I think you've seen enough of the cream jacket and trousers.'

Her eyes ran up and down his body. It was amazing how that tiny act could make his hairs stand on end and make him feel distinctly hot under the collar.

She gave an approving nod. 'I like it,' she said as she stepped away. 'I like it even more that you didn't bother with a tie.' She spun towards him in her heels. 'I never did like a man in a tie.'

His heart leapt in his chest. Her mood was lifting. She was definitely beginning to relax. He caught her elbow and spun her back towards him, resting his other hand on her hip.

He wanted this to be the start of something new. He wanted a chance to make things work with the only woman he'd ever really loved.

He knew they both had to move on. He knew they might not be able to move on together. And he knew at some point they had to talk about Ariella Rose.

But his heart was squeezing in his chest.

Tonight could be perfect. Tonight could just be about them. And somehow he knew that if he gave her the guarantee of no pressure, it could change everything.

'What do you say that for tonight I promise you that I won't mention Ariella Rose. We won't talk about what happened. And we'll only concentrate on the here and now. We'll only concentrate on the good things.'

He slid his hand through her silky soft hair.

She'd outlined her eyes in black and put on some lipstick that matched her dress. Right now Lucia was every bit the Italian siren.

Tonight wasn't about upsetting her. Tonight wasn't about grieving.

Tonight was about reminding her how good things had been between them. Reminding her what it felt like to truly connect with a person— and hoping she might realise that some things were worth fighting for.

She blinked quickly, trying to lose the obvious sheen on her eyes. Her voice was shaky. 'You promise?'

'I promise.' He didn't hesitate. This was the only way. The only way to try and take the steps to move forward. He wouldn't leave Venice without having that conversation with her but for tonight—just for tonight—he wanted to capture just a little of the old Lucia and Logan again.

She locked up the apartment and they headed downstairs. He gestured her towards the other entrance of the building, the one that looked out over the Grand Canal and had a private mooring dock.

She shook her head. 'We never use that any more.'

He smiled as he pulled at the older doors. 'Well, tonight we're going to.'

Her stomach had been doing little flip-flops since early afternoon and didn't seem to want to stop any time soon.

The dress he'd bought her was beautiful, elegant without being revealing and still managing to fit like a second skin. It might as well have been made especially for her.

When she'd put it on she'd felt a surge of confidence she hadn't felt in years. And seeing Logan in his dark suit had almost toppled her off the edge where she was dangling. It was like recapturing a moment from twelve years ago, when they'd used to dress up regularly and go out eating and dancing together. Back when neither had had a care in the world and she'd had no idea what could lie ahead.

Logan's green eyes were twinkling as he opened the door to the Grand Canal. Bobbing on the water was a sleek black gondola edged in red and gilt with its own private canopy.

Lucia sucked in a breath. 'What on earth have you done?' She knew exactly how much these cost to hire. Every night the Grand Canal was full of wide-eyed tourists bobbing around in these private hired gondolas. Most of the local Venetians laughed at them being taken advantage of. She'd never guessed Logan would fall into the trap.

'I've decided to start this evening the way it should continue.' He was smiling and his voice was steady. She could swear the orange-bathed canal was almost shimmering behind him. It made the whole evening just seem a little magical.

She glanced down at her towering stilettos as

the gondolier held out his hand towards her. Her footsteps were slightly tottery as she stepped over the dark water of the Grand Canal. While it could seem terribly romantic, she didn't want to land in it and re-emerge like a creature of the black lagoon.

Logan jumped over easily, catching hold of her waist and steering her towards the red velvet love seat on the gondola. She laughed as they plonked down onto the seat under a black canopy and the gondola started gliding along the canal.

It was the first time in her life she'd felt like a tourist in Venice. Logan's arm slid easily behind her back. The love seat was unsurprisingly small, making sure they sat snugly together, his leg touching the length of hers.

It had been years and years since she'd done anything like this.

There was something magical about Venice in the early evening. Voices were hushed, music floated through the air, and quiet had fallen over the city.

'This is lovely,' Lucia murmured. Logan gave her shoulder a little squeeze.

As she watched the world go by she started to relax into his hold. He'd promised her there would be no pressure, no tension tonight. A tiny part of her coiled-up stomach didn't exactly believe him. It was hard to be around Logan and not think about Ariella Rose at all—and she was sure he must feel the same way.

But for tonight it might be nice not to focus on the hurts of the past. It hadn't been Logan who had hurt her. She'd never felt let down by him, or felt animosity towards him.

He was just the biggest reminder of Ariella Rose, and until her head could get around that...

The gondolier moved smoothly through the traffic. She had no idea where they were going but it was obvious he was going the picturesque route, winding their way through lesser canals and under bridges. She could see tourists pointing and taking pictures. Thank goodness for the canopy as it gave some ounce of privacy without spoiling their view.

There was something nice about the sound of

the water lapping gently at the side of the gondola. Logan took his arm from her shoulder and bent forward, bringing out a bottle of chilled Prosecco and two glasses. He popped the cork and filled them up, handing hers over and holding his towards her. 'Here's to a fabulous night in Venice.'

She clinked her glass against his and sipped, letting the bubbles explode across her tongue and tickle her nose. 'Here's to an unusual night in Venice,' she said.

He raised his eyebrows. 'You mean you don't travel by gondola every night?'

She shook her head. 'I mean I haven't travelled in a gondola *ever* since I got here.'

'Really?' He seemed surprised.

She shrugged her shoulders. 'Think of it this way. If you lived in Pisa, how many times would you actually climb the tower?'

He wrinkled his brow. 'I get where you're coming from but this is me—remember?' He turned a little more to face her. She could see the faint shadow on his jawline. He'd probably only shaved a few hours ago but that didn't quell the rapid growth of his potential beard. Her fingers itched to reach out and touch.

Logan wasn't finished. 'Remember when we stayed in Florence? How many times did we keep visiting the baptistery at the Duomo or stand underneath the Renaissance dome?'

She shook her head. 'That's because you're an architect junkie and those things were right on our doorstep.' She raised her eyebrows at him. 'I do remember you found a way to charm guards at every attraction and skip the queues.'

He gave a wave of his hand and glanced at her mischievously. 'There's a reason Italian men were born with charm. Anyway, we were natives. The guards knew that.'

'Only because you slipped some money in their hands.'

He gave a deep laugh. 'I don't know what you're taking about.' There were crinkles around his green eyes and her heart gave a little lurch.

Logan Cascini was really every woman's dream guy. She'd forgotten just how much fun they used to have together. It was unusual to meet a guy who shared her passion for the arts as much as he did.

From what most of her girlfriends told her, it was unusual to feel so connected, so in tune with a guy as she had with Logan. Most of her friends went for tempestuous and volatile relationships with plates smashing and clothes being tossed out of windows.

Life with Logan had been passionate but fulfilling. Something she'd never found again.

The gondola slid up next to the service point for disembarkation. It rocked precariously as she tried to stand up and she wobbled as the gondolier leapt ashore and held his hand out towards her.

As her feet landed on steady ground she turned towards Logan again. They were right at the edge of Piazza San Marco—the busiest place in Venice. The crowds might be a little quieter because of the planned concert but it was buzzing with excitement.

'Ready?'

He nodded towards the gondolier, tipped him and slid an arm around her waist, steering her towards the Procuraties. The sun was even lower in the sky now. The Procuraties were lit at night with tiny white lights. It was like a thousand glittering candles flickering in the night. There was no denying the beauty of the setting.

Music drifted down towards them. Some of these restaurants were known as the finest in the world, with Michelin-starred chefs and award-winning menus.

He pointed to a set of stairs heading up towards Rubins. 'After you.'

She felt her stomach flip over. He was being so formal around her. So controlled. The tiny bit of laughter on the boat had been the one true time she'd glimpsed the real Logan. That was who she wanted to spend the evening with.

The restaurant was beautiful. White linen tablecloths, more flickering candles and a harpist playing in the corner. It was full of couples dining in the dimmed lights, capturing a moment in one of the most beautiful cities in the world.

Logan held out her chair as she sat at the table then ordered them some wine. The waiter gave them thick, leather-covered menus. Lucia gave a smile as the wine appeared and was poured. 'It looks like we could have finished the wine by the time we get through this menu.'

Logan smiled at the waiter and closed his menu. 'What do you recommend?'

In the end they ordered a mixture of duck stuffed ravioli, white truffle pasta, fish carpaccio and some veal escalopes with Dobbiaco cheese.

The food was delicious and the wine kept flowing, almost as much as the easy chatter.

'What do you have to work on after the Tuscany project?'

Logan smiled at her. 'I could tell you, but I might have to kill you.' He tapped the side of his nose.

She leaned forward. 'Oh, don't go all James Bond on me. Is it something good?'

He leaned forward too, his voice low. 'It's something great. I'm just waiting for the final word. Let's just say I'll be working on something in Rome. Something I would absolutely love to work on and which could really put my restoration business under the spotlight.'

'Doesn't the chapel and *palazzo* restoration in Tuscany already do that? I'd have thought the royal wedding would mean everyone involved would benefit from the publicity.'

He gave a sigh. 'It does. But this is different, this is real Renaissance architecture. Something special that's needed to be restored for a number of years.'

She shook her head as she kept eating the delicious food. 'You make it sound like my dream job of being asked to restore the Michelangelo frescoes.'

'It's close.'

She almost dropped her fork. 'Really?'

He nodded. 'They are considering a number of different companies. The work definitely needs to be done, it just depends who wins the contract.'

She frowned. She knew just how passionate Logan was about his work, just how particular. 'There can't be many firms that have as good a reputation as you have.'

He met her gaze. 'Thanks for the compliment.

Any chance you could be on the selection committee?'

She threw back her head and laughed. The wine was starting to kick in. The venue was exquisite and the food delicious. As for the company…

Logan put down his knife and fork. 'Honestly, what would you do if you got asked to do some restoration work on one of Michelangelo's frescoes?'

His face was completely serious. What on earth had he been asked to do?

'Honestly? I would probably die of shock. And I would be too scared to even contemplate doing something like that.'

He tilted his head. 'But you work for the Italian Heritage Board. Isn't that exactly the place that should be asked to do these things?'

She shook her head. 'We're just one organisation. I would be terrified. The pressure would be overwhelming and the criticism—before I even started—would be even more so.' She sat back in her chair. 'When it comes to things like that, I prefer just to admire along with the rest of the general public.'

'And Burano?'

She shook her head. 'His work isn't as well known. Isn't as criticised. The Madonna and Child hasn't been seen in generations. It isn't even on official records. Restoring it to its former beauty will be an act of joy.'

She could see him suck in a breath at her words. He paused, then looked up between heavy lids, 'And do you think everything can be restored—even people?'

Her skin chilled and her throat closed over. It was almost as if someone had stood behind her and poured icy water over her head.

He'd promised. He'd promised he wouldn't mention this tonight. She stood up swiftly, her chair toppling over behind her.

Logan was on his feet in an instant. It was almost as if he'd realised what had slipped out of his mouth. He walked swiftly over to the waiter, thrusting a bundle of notes at him.

Lucia didn't wait, she turned on her impossibly high heels and took off down the stairs.

But Piazza San Marco wasn't ready to give up on her yet.

As they'd had dinner, a small string quintet had been setting up downstairs outside one of the neighbouring restaurants. With the whole square bathed in flickering lights, the silhouette of the Basilica and Clock Tower at one end and the outlined string players in the middle her feet came to an abrupt halt.

Even she knew that running through the middle of a quintet in the piazza wasn't her best idea.

As she sucked in some air to try and still her thudding heart, she felt a presence behind her. Logan's hand slid across the thin red fabric of the dress covering her belly. She felt his warm breath on her shoulder and he moved in gently, letting her feel the rise and fall of his chest against her shoulder blades.

She was upset. But she wasn't angry at his touch. Instead, it felt like a comfort blanket.

Two of the violinists lifted their instruments and the quintet started to play. It wasn't what she expected. Classical music—usually opera—was often heard in the piazza. But this was different. It was a modern song by a UK male singer, transformed and made beautiful by the strings. She could almost hear his words echoing about love and loss in her ears.

It was almost as if they knew exactly what to play.

She spun around, placing her hands flat on Logan's chest. He didn't say a word, just lifted one hand and let his finger trail down her cheek until it reached her shoulder, where he flicked her curls back.

He was watching her with those steady green eyes and she could see the hurt shimmering from him. He was trying so hard, but was finding this every bit as difficult as she was.

His other hand slid around her hips, halting at her lower spine.

They were locked together. Just the way they should be.

Her palms slid up the planes of his chest and rested on his shoulders. This was her Logan. No one else's. No one else could ever come close to the connection she felt with him.

His body started to sway, tiny movements from side to side. One hand stayed at the base of her spine and the other tangled through her hair.

Dancing. She hadn't danced since…

Since before she'd had Ariella Rose.

She and Logan had once danced all the time. Sometimes in the clubs of Florence, often at family events and sometimes in the privacy of their own home.

Most of all she'd just loved the feeling of being in his arms and the warm touch of his body next to hers.

As the melody moved past the introduction he reached up and captured her hand in his, leading her away from the stairs and onto the patterned floor of Piazza San Marco. Little lights glowed under their feet.

People were still walking past, stopping to listen to the music, with one other couple dancing nearby.

He turned her to face her, putting his hands on her hips. 'Ready to recapture the past, Lucia?' he whispered.

She reached up and put her hand on his chest again. She could feel his warm skin and beating heart underneath the fine Italian shirt.

All she could focus on was the way he was looking at her. It made her feel like the only girl on the planet.

She slid her hands around his neck and rested her head against his chest. 'Always,' she replied.

Their footsteps moved in perfect unison. The warmth of his body next to hers felt overwhelming.

They fitted so well together it almost felt like they'd never been apart. And Logan didn't just know how to sway to the music. He knew how to dance—how to really dance.

It was as if they could read each other's minds and knew exactly what the next steps should be. She moved her hand from his chest, sliding it along the length of his arm and letting their hands clasp.

She felt him stiffen against her and she lifted her head.

There was no doubt on his face. He released her from his grasp against him and spun her outwards. When she danced with Logan she always felt like she could fly.

He could lift and spin her as if she were as light as air. Her dress spun out, the ripples of red fabric twisting high from her thighs, the stiletto heels forgotten as she continued to follow his lead.

She could hear the murmurs around them as people stopped to stare. But all she could focus on was the beat of the music and the feel of Logan's hard muscles as they connected briefly through the parts of the music.

Logan knew how to lead. He knew how to steer her and how to whip her around, like a matador with a cape.

And she kept spinning. The lit arches of the Procuraties flashing past her line of vision. The evening was still warm and her body temperature was rising quickly.

She couldn't even begin to think straight. The only thing that counted was how right everything felt—how *connected* everything felt.

She dipped her head and spun under his arm three times as the crowd gasped. The momentum of the music was building. He caught her around the waist and dipped her backwards. It was one of their all-time favourite moves. The sensuality of the deep arch of her back, followed by her ever-so-slow stretch back up, ending up nose to nose with Logan.

He was breathing just as quickly as she was. A laugh escaped from her lips. Her hair fell over her face, some of her curls connecting with his skin. But he didn't brush them back, he just dipped his head further forward, allowing them both to be hidden beneath the veil of her hair.

'How are we doing?' he murmured. He ran one finger up her spine, sending shock waves everywhere, a thousand beautiful butterflies beating their wings against her skin.

It couldn't be more perfect than this.

Then he moved. The music was slowing, reaching a building crescendo. He spun her once more, letting her skirt billow around her and her hair stream outwards.

He caught her hips suddenly, stopping her in mid-pivot and pressing his head against hers.

She didn't even have time to catch her breath before his lips were on hers.

There was no time to think about where they were or what they had been doing. There was no time to think about the audience or the scenery.

His hands skirted around her behind, her hips and up the sides of her waist, stopping as they tangled in her hair, and he anchored her head firmly in one hand.

She couldn't ever remember being kissed like this—even by Logan.

She couldn't get enough of him. His taste, his smell, the feel of his body beneath the palms of her hand. He was hers. He was all hers. And she didn't want this to stop.

He pulled his lips back from hers, staying close enough to let her feel his breath on her skin. 'It's you, Lucia. It's always been you.'

The music died around them, but she hardly noticed. Her heartbeat was roaring in her ears. The world around them was still spinning—just like her brain. It hadn't stopped. Not for a second.

Logan held her tightly to him. She could feel

his knotted muscles, the tension as he held her. She had no doubt about the effects she had on his body.

Of the effects he had on hers.

It had been so long. She'd forgotten what passion like this felt like. Something had been ignited inside her. A tiny flame that had been dimmed for so long. Now the fire was burning so brightly she couldn't imagine putting it out again.

Logan's eyes fixed on hers. They were steady but had never seemed so determined—so heated.

He clasped one hand in his. 'Let's go.' He didn't wait for a response. He walked away briskly, pulling her behind him as he parted the crowd around them.

His long strides covered the expanse of Piazza San Marco easily, and she was running in her stilettos to keep up.

She was surprised to see the sleek, black gondola still waiting. He didn't wait for the chatting gondolier to pay attention, just turned and lifted her straight onto the swaying gondola, shouting an instruction to the gondolier.

With one tug the canopy was closed, leaving them in a pool of darkness, with only a few of Venice's lights flickering behind them.

A seed of doubt flashed through her brain. All the rational thoughts that she'd completely ignored for the last few hours started to take seed and let their roots unfurl. She couldn't stop the rapid thud-thud of her heart. Every inch of her skin was on fire, the tiny hairs on her arms standing on end.

Her eyes started to adjust to the dim light. Logan hadn't moved. It could only have been a few seconds, but it felt like so much longer. It felt as if his brain must be crowding with the same doubts that she was feeling. Her stomach clenched. Everything suddenly felt like a huge mistake.

Logan shifted his body towards hers, reaching up his hand towards her face. He ran one finger across her forehead. Her eyes automatically closed and the finger traced down over her eyelids, cheeks, across her lips then under her chin and to the tender skin of her décolletage.

He leaned closer, the heat from his body spreading towards hers.

And then he murmured those words again.

'It's you Lucia, it's always been you.'

Before, she'd been shocked. They'd been in the middle of Piazza San Marco with a crowd of onlookers. Here, it was entirely private. All she could hear was the movement of the gondola slipping through the waters of Venice.

She squeezed her eyes closed again for a few seconds. Her hand reached up towards him. She couldn't help it. She couldn't be this close to Logan and not touch him. It was all she could think about.

She felt him suck in a breath as she ran the palm of her hand along his now-stubbled jaw.

If she could suspend the past—suspend the memories—then everything about Logan was perfect.

Now, as he said the words it was just the two of them. Her heart wanted to melt. Her lips wanted to respond. She wanted to say it had only ever been him. She wanted to tell him that she'd never felt the same about anyone else—she *couldn't* feel the same about anyone else.

Without Logan she wasn't living. She was only existing.

She didn't want to just exist any more.

This time when he bent to kiss her she matched him move for move. She ran her hands through his dark hair and pulled him closer to her, pressing her breasts against his chest.

Logan knew how to kiss. He really knew how to kiss. There was a zing as their lips met. Teeth grazed her lips. Then his lips were firmly on hers. Tasting her, caressing her. Full sweet lips on hers, filling her with so much promise, so much expectation.

The zings didn't stop at her lips but carried on right around her body, like an army on rapid attack. She couldn't help her responses. She couldn't help but push harder against his body, her hands exploring his back and shoulders.

The kiss intensified with every passing second, sparking a whole host of memories throughout her body. It didn't matter that their eyes were closed. With this kiss Logan could see every part of her, burrow his way to the centre of her closed-over soul.

She'd always felt threatened by their closeness after the death of their daughter. Fear had pushed her into a position of retreat, because even though she'd told Logan she couldn't talk about things, once he'd kissed her she always felt at her most vulnerable. Her most open.

His earthy scent swam around her. His fingers stroked the back of her neck, giving her a promise of what was to come.

His kisses moved lower, along her cheek and down the delicate skin of her neck. For a moment she almost objected. She didn't want his lips to leave hers.

But Logan knew all her secret places. Knew the tiny spot at the back of her ear that made her gasp with pleasure and lose all rational thought. Before she'd even thought about it her head was arching backwards, opening up the more sensitive skin at the bottom of her throat.

And Logan didn't hesitate. He was on it in a flash. She wanted to move. Her dress was inching upwards, his hand brushing against her thighs. But space was cramped under the canopy, with nowhere really to go, and they both jumped apart as the gondola jerked suddenly as it scraped against wood.

She sat back in the love seat, trying to still her ragged breaths. There was another couple of bumps.

It had been deliberate. Of course it had. They'd reached their destination and their gondolier had enough experience to allow his guests a moment of warning.

Was this it? Was this where this evening ended?

Logan pulled back the canopy and stood up, straightening his rumpled jacket and shirt and then turning towards her. He didn't speak, just held out his hand towards her.

What happened next was up to her.

It was her apartment. Her space. She'd offered him somewhere to stay for the weekend, without even considering this as a possibility.

The sun had set now. The warm orange glow from earlier had disappeared.

But now Venice was alive with a million different lights brightening up the almost black sky. Logan was outlined like a film star on his final movie shot.

The backdrop was stunning with the beautiful architecture along the Grand Canal and silhouetted gondolas around them.

But all she could focus on was Logan.

Because she knew exactly how this night would end.

It was already written in the stars twinkling in the sky above their head.

She slid her hand into his and he pulled her towards him as the boat rocked on the water.

This was fate. It had to be.

And who was she to fight fate?

CHAPTER EIGHT

THE ROOM WAS bathed in the pale light of morning.

It wasn't what he expected—not at all. Last night he hadn't paid attention to anything around them. They'd barely managed to close the apartment door behind them before they'd stumbled through to her bedroom.

Lucia's room wasn't the stark white of the guest bedroom along the corridor. It was sumptuous and opulent, furnished in the colours she'd used to favour when painting. Purples and golds with a tiny flash of red. It suited the general feel of the apartment—the whole place still had the hint of a palace about it. And the beautiful décor and furnishings in the room were more personal— more Lucia—than the room he'd stayed in.

Lucia was still tangled in his arms, her head resting on his chest and her dark locks fanned out on the purple bedding. Her breathing was slow and steady. The early morning light and noise from the Grand Canal hadn't woken her yet.

He didn't want to move. Didn't want to breathe in case it disturbed her.

This was perfection. This was exactly the way things should be between them but he knew he would have to destroy it all.

It would be so easy. So easy to say nothing at all and ignore the huge elephant that sat in the corner of the room every time they were together. But Logan didn't want only part of Lucia. He wanted all of her. He'd waited this long. And if he couldn't have all of her...

His hand reached up and stroked her head. They would have to spend the next few months working together in Tuscany. They could flirt, laugh, love and sleep together and make a poor attempt at having a relationship.

But the truth was that any attempt would be futile until they'd spoken about Ariella Rose. They had to start from scratch. They could only build this relationship once they'd grieved together for their daughter. And he still didn't know if Lucia was capable of that.

His phone beeped on the table next to the bed. The noise stirred Lucia from her peaceful sleep and she woke gradually.

Her arm drifted across his chest. She was smiling as she woke, as if she were in the middle of some alluring dream.

Her eyelids flickered open, revealing her dark brown eyes surrounded by thick black lashes. All traces of last night's make-up had vanished. Lucia didn't need any. Her flawless skin and naturally red lips were enticing enough.

His stomach clenched as he waited for anything—any trace of regret about last night. 'Good morning, beautiful,' he said softly.

She smiled and closed her eyes again, pushing her naked body closer to his. Her fingers started tracing circles on his chest. 'Good morning, handsome,' she said sleepily.

Some of his tension dissipated. He could leave this. Say nothing. Stroke his fingers across her skin and pull her beneath the covers. It was the biggest temptation in the world right now.

And while it might offer some temporary sanctuary and pleasure it wouldn't take him to the place he ultimately wanted to be.

Somehow he knew it didn't matter how he phrased the question—he already knew how she would react.

It was horrible—knowing that the path they would have to tread would be a painful one. But he was ready for it. He'd been ready for it for the past twelve years.

'How are you feeling?'

She pushed her head up onto one hand as she lay facing him. Her face still had that relaxed, sleepy, dreamy quality about it. It was the most chilled he'd ever seen her.

'I'm fine.' She smiled. 'How are you?' There was a teasing tone to her voice—as if she wanted to take this to a whole other place.

His fingers wanted to reach out and touch her soft skin. It took all his will power not to move and instead to clench the purple sheet in his fist.

'We need to talk, Lucia. You know we need to talk.'

The muscles around her neck tensed. She turned her head away from him. 'No, we don't.'

It was an immediate, instinctual reaction. He knew that. He pushed himself further up the bed. The sheet moved with him, pulling from Lucia's skin. She made a grab for it. It was amazing how a few words could make you feel naked all over again.

He sighed. 'We have to work together, Lucia. We're going to be in Tuscany together. I don't want things to be awkward between us.'

Her head shot around. 'And this is how you stop it?' It was an accusatory tone. And he got that. He did. Lucia would much rather they never spoke about this at all.

He moved to the edge of the bed and picked up his discarded shirt from the floor, pulling it over his head. He shook his head. 'No, Lucia. This is how I start things. This is how we should start things. By talking.' He stood up. 'Now get dressed. We're going to go for breakfast together.'

He moved across the floor, finding his underwear, crumpled trousers and shoes. If he were a young man, concerned about his appearance, he might be cringing right now at the thought of going out in Venice in last night's clothes.

But he was a grown-up. An adult. And he had so much more to worry about.

Lucia was scowling at him. The beautiful red dress he'd bought her was bunched up in a little ball. He doubted it would ever look the same. 'I'm not coming.'

'Yes, you are.' He opened the door of her wardrobe, his eyes running rapidly over the colours, and pulled out a flowered dress, throwing it on the bed. 'Would you like me to select your underwear too?' He didn't mean to be cruel. But he wasn't prepared to take no for an answer. Not after all this time.

She pulled the sheet up under her chin. 'Stop it, Logan. You can't bully me into doing what you want. I'm not a child.'

He bent down next to her. 'I have never bullied you, Lucia. I never will. And you're right, you're not a child. You're a mother—just like I'm a father. Just because our child isn't here any more it doesn't change that.'

Her eyes widened. She was shocked. It was the last thing she'd obviously expected to hear. And he wasn't quite sure where it had come from.

After a few seconds her fingers released on the sheet a little. He sensed the moment and opened the drawer next to her bed, pulling out matching white underwear. 'I'll give you a few minutes to get dressed,' he said, walking to the door and standing in the corridor.

Every part of him was on edge. He had no idea right now if he'd handled this right. He'd spent so long tiptoeing around Lucia that now it felt as if he'd just leapt in wearing a pair of clown-size shoes.

He held his breath, listening for any sign of movement. Any tiny noise.

After a few seconds he heard something. The gentle movement of a sheet. He leaned back against the wall. It didn't matter that she hated him right now. All that mattered was that they talk. That they *really* talked.

He walked through to the guest bedroom and quickly washed his face and hands, running his fingers through his hair and brushing his teeth. He had another shirt in his bag but it would probably be equally as rumpled. He hadn't planned on staying in Venice so clothes were definitely scarce.

It was too warm for a jacket so he walked through to the main room and waited for Lucia to appear.

It only took a few moments. She hadn't bothered with make-up and her hair was pulled back in a clasp. The yellow and pink flowered dress made her look much younger.

His heartbeat turned up a little notch. It was almost like turning back time. She had a white canvas bag in her hand and some flat sandals on her feet. But she'd never looked so beautiful.

He walked over to the main door and held it open. 'Let's go.'

There was a sinking feeling in his stomach. Almost as if he knew how this could turn out.

Lucia didn't even glance at him as she walked past. She had that determined edge to her chin.

But he could be equally determined. It was time to show her how much.

* * *

Talk about an awkward morning after. She couldn't believe she'd allowed herself to get into this position.

She knew so much better than this.

She was an adult and knew exactly what going for dinner and wine with Logan could lead to. The sexual chemistry between them had always been off the chart, but add into that the dress-buying and dancing and, well…what chance had she really had?

She held her head up proudly as she walked down the street towards her favourite café. This wasn't like doing a walk of shame the next day after a night-time encounter.

Logan had been the man she'd lived with. He'd been the man who'd cherished and treasured her. He'd been the man she'd loved with her whole heart.

She still did.

Her feet stumbled on the uneven street. Logan caught her elbow and she tugged it away. Where had that thought come from?

She squeezed her eyes closed for a second.

This was because of last night. Memories of what had been and how good they had been together. She was being sentimental, nothing more. So why was her stomach permanently in knots?

She stopped at the tables on the street at her favourite café. Logan pulled out a chair for her. The waiter gave her a wave. 'Usual?'

She nodded. Logan caught his eye 'Make it two.'

Little parts of her were starting to unravel, even at those innocuous words. Logan knew that her usual would be coffee with steamed milk and a heated croissant with raspberry jam. He knew her that well and was happy to eat the same as her.

It was almost as if he were chipping away at the barriers she'd erected around herself all those years ago. The ones that had protected her. Stopped her from getting too close to anyone else and kept her safe from being hurt.

Logan folded his arms across his chest. He was sitting directly opposite her, his eyes watching her carefully.

He waited until the coffee appeared on the table and the waft of buttery croissants filled the air around them.

'It's been too long, Lucia,' he said quietly. 'I never wanted you to leave, but I understood you needed time and space.' He picked up his spoon and stirred his coffee. 'But it was never my intention to leave things this long.'

He had no idea what those few words could do to her.

The rest of Venice seemed completely at ease. People were laughing and strolling in the early Sunday morning light. Shopkeepers were just starting to roll up their shutters and open their doors. A street vendor wandered past, clutching buckets filled with beautiful flowers. The assorted scents started to mix with that of the breakfast croissants. It could be a beautiful day. So why did it feel like the worst?

Logan hadn't finished talking. 'I always hoped things would be different. I thought you would be married. I thought you would be a mother.' He paused. 'I always hoped you would be.'

She felt tears spring to her eyes. It was almost

as if he were twisting the knife that was currently piercing her heart. She knew that wasn't his intention. She knew he was trying his best to move things forward.

But Lucia had never moved forward. She could remember everything about Ariella Rose as if it had just happened yesterday. She could remember the sudden unexpected pain, the cramps, the awkward delivery. She could remember the tiny fragile bundle. Ariella had been so small she could fit in one hand, wrapped in a pink blanket made by Nonna.

The almost transparent skin. The tiny little blue veins underneath. She could remember how she'd had to gently ease up a tiny eyelid in order to see her baby's eyes. Eyes that would never see the world.

Lungs that would never fill with air.

She could remember all her hopes and dreams for the future evaporate with the silence in the air. The heavy, ominous silence of nothing.

Her horror had been so complete she'd only been able to shed a few tears. Tears of shock. It had been as if every emotion in her body had switched off. Gone into complete self-protection mode.

Now Logan was trying to open her all up to this again.

'Maybe I decided that wasn't what I wanted.' The words came out tight, almost angry, and Logan eyebrows arched slowly.

'You were made to be a mother, Lucia.' He held her gaze as she tried to swallow. 'You would be the finest mother in the world.'

She was frozen. Couldn't breathe. Her mouth had never felt so dry, but the aroma of coffee was acrid to her now. The croissant mocked her.

Some modern career women would find his words insulting. But she didn't. Logan knew her better than anyone. He knew how much she'd relished being pregnant. He knew how much she'd planned for their daughter—they both had.

Although she was passionate about her career, she'd longed to raise their daughter.

She lifted her coffee cup with trembling hands. 'Things change.'

He shook his head and reached across the table towards her.

But she didn't want him to touch her. She couldn't take the feel of his skin on hers right now.

He leaned his elbows on the table and just kept talking. 'I've dreamt of being a father too. But it's never happened. It wasn't meant to happen—not with anyone but you.'

He said the words so easily. As if he'd contemplated them for a long time and had come to accept that this was his lot in life.

'I've met some wonderful women, but none that I wanted to marry, none that I wanted to raise children with. I only ever wanted to do that with you.'

She could feel the anger build in her chest. 'But we never planned Ariella Rose. You make it sound as if we had our future all written out.' She spat the words at him.

She couldn't understand how he could talk about any of this so calmly. It felt as if he'd reached a fist into her chest and was squeezing all the blood from her pumping heart.

'My future was written the second I saw you,

Lucia.' He hadn't raised his voice once. His words were calm and steady. He was so resolute.

She leaned across the table towards him. 'I can't talk about this,' she hissed.

It was the first time she saw a little spark in him. He gritted his teeth. 'Well, you have to. It's about time. You owe it to our daughter.'

She pulled back as if he'd wounded her. But Logan wasn't finished. 'You owe it to our daughter to talk about her and give her the love and respect she deserves.'

Her head was swimming. 'How dare you! You know I loved Ariella.'

'But you don't honour her memory.'

'What does that mean?'

Logan rubbed the palms of his hand on his trousers. It was obvious this was upsetting him just as much as it was upsetting her.

He took a deep breath. 'It means you walked away, Lucia. You walked away from the memory of our daughter and the memory of what we used to have. I think about her every single day. It doesn't matter that you're in Venice and she's in Tuscany. I visit her grave every month.

You could too. But as far as I know you haven't been there since the day we buried her.'

Fury erupted inside her. Tears were brimming in her eyes but they just couldn't come any further—she hadn't been able to cry since the day they'd buried their daughter. From that point on everything had been locked inside.

'I can't go there. I can't visit.'

'Why?' He wouldn't stop. He wasn't going to let this go. It would have been better if they'd never seen each other again. The last thing she needed was stirring up the memories of Ariella Rose and any association with Logan did just that.

She wasn't able to separate the parts of him from their daughter. She couldn't just remember his kiss, his touch without remembering where it had led them. Couldn't block out all the pain it had caused.

'I just can't.'

'Then maybe that's what we should do.'

She felt herself bristle. 'Don't tell me what to do, Logan. We haven't known each other in a long time—you have no right.'

He stood up sharply, his chair screeching backwards, and she held her breath, wondering what would come next. The waiter stuck his head out of the door of the restaurant, watching carefully.

But Logan just shook his head, stretched out his back, then took a few steps towards her and knelt beside her chair.

She was still holding her breath as he slid his hand up and took hers. She hadn't realised it but her hands were cold and the warmth from him completely enveloped her.

His voice was quiet again, this time almost pleading. 'I have every right. We lost our daughter together. Who do you think I get to talk about Ariella Rose with? Who do I get to share the memories of our daughter with? I want to remember what we lost, Lucia. I loved her with every part of my heart—just as you did.' He sighed and looked up, meeting her gaze.

'This isn't just about you any more, Lucia. It was twelve years ago. I would have done anything to help you grieve, to comfort you after the loss of our daughter. But I've realised this is about me too. It wasn't enough just to make the arrangements. It wasn't enough to say a prayer. It wasn't about giving you the space you needed. I watched you fall apart right under my nose, I watched you shut yourself off from the world and bury yourself away. I thought I had no right to force you to talk. I thought I had to let you do this your own way. But twelve years on? I was wrong, Lucia. I was very wrong. For you, and for me.'

She squeezed her eyes closed again. She couldn't take his intense and sincere glance. This was exactly what she'd always tried to avoid.

It had been too much. Too much to think about. She couldn't bear it.

And now here was Logan—her strong, able Logan—telling her how much he'd been hurt too. He'd never worn his heart so much on his sleeve as he was doing now and it was tearing her apart.

She'd never even contemplated his hurt. His grief. She'd been too selfishly trying to cope with her own. Logan had appeared so composed, so strong. Now his face looked as if it had worn a river of grief across it. She could see her own pain reflected in his eyes, the tight grip of her hand telling her more than she wanted to know.

'You have to face this, Lucia. You're never going to get past this, *I'm* never going to get past this, if we can't talk together.'

Logan. Her handsome, strong Logan. She'd always hoped he would have married and had kids. He deserved to be a father. He deserved to spend his summer evenings playing in a garden, with his arms wrapped around the woman that he loved.

Twelve years ago she'd hoped that might be her.

He still wanted to save her. Even after all these years he wanted to patch her up and put her together again. But he couldn't do it then. And he couldn't do it now.

But things were different now. He'd realised how much *he* still hurt.

It didn't matter if Lucia wrapped her arms around his neck right now and told him she wanted to try and make things work again. It didn't matter that she might want a future with them together.

Now he'd realised exactly what he needed. For him. And for her.

He lifted his hand then ran his fingers through her hair at the side of her head. 'I loved Ariella Rose. I loved it that her eyes were so dark blue, though they probably would have turned brown—just like yours. I loved the fine downy hair we could see on her head. I loved that her fingers and toes were perfect. I dream about the person she could have become. And I wonder about the type of personality she would have had.'

He moved his fingers down her cheek. 'I wonder if she would have been like me, or if she would have been like you.'

He brought his hand down next to his other, clasping both of her hands in his. 'I love it that we made a little person. But I watch the calendar every year. Every year when it's her birthday I think about another year that we've lost. I think about the little girl who would have grown up and laughed and played and gone to school. I think she would be at an age right now where she would hate her overprotective dad. She would hate the fact I didn't want her to speak to boys or to wear clothes that made her look like a teenager. I would want to keep her all buttoned up in pink dresses and sandals.'

Lucia was shaking. And not just her hands. Every part of her body was shaking. It was as if his words were starting to penetrate her fortress-like exterior.

He could see the waiter casting anxious glances in their direction. But he didn't want to do anything that might distract her.

'Tell me how much you miss her, Lucia. Tell me what your hopes and dreams were for our daughter.'

He couldn't do anything to stop the shaking. He knew it was just her body's natural response. He just kept her ice-cold hands in his, hoping and praying she would finally start to open up.

Her voice was tight. Her fingers started to grip his hand more tightly. Almost as if she were clinging on for her life.

'I miss her every day.' The words came out in a rush. Then there was silence. Silence he was determined not to fill. It was the first time she'd ever said anything about their daughter.

Lucia finally started to talk again. 'I get so angry because I don't know whether she would have had dark hair, or blond hair like your sisters. I don't know whether she would have had curls or straight hair. I don't know whether she would have been a tomboy or a ballet dancer. Whether she would have wanted red shoes or pink or white.' She shook her head. 'There's so many things about my daughter that I don't know. Will never know. And I feel cheated, completely and utterly cheated.'

His chest was tight. But tiny little parts of the tightness were giving away to relief. She was finally, finally starting to talk. Starting to talk about the life they had lost.

'Then I think about things that would never, ever have mattered. Not in the scale of things.' She looked upwards to the sky.

'What do you mean?' he prompted gently.

'I mean, would she have liked cats or dogs?

Would she have been artistic? Would she have liked staying in Florence? How would she have got on at school? All the things that—if our daughter was actually here—we probably would have argued about and fussed over. But in the end, it doesn't mean anything.' Her eyes lowered and fixed on the canal next to the café. A few boats were puttering past. People going about their daily business.

No one else could know or imagine what was at stake at this table.

Logan took a deep breath. He had so much more to say. Even though he'd been much more able to talk about his grief than Lucia, there was something about it just being the two of them here that made it different.

No one else could really understand how they both felt—not unless they'd lost a child too.

He straightened up and sat back down in the chair opposite her again. But this time he pulled it closer, away from the table and round to the side so their legs were touching.

'I miss things,' he said softly. 'I miss us. I miss

what we used to have together. I didn't just lose a daughter, Lucia. I lost the love of my life too.'

He could see her swallow painfully. It wasn't just him that felt this way. But somehow Lucia didn't want to go there. It was as if, now she'd finally managed to say something about Ariella, she didn't know how to stop.

'Sometimes I think we were lucky. Sometimes I think that I'm selfish.'

His head shot up in surprise. 'What?'

She scrunched up her face. Her voice was sad. 'I look at other people who've lost children. You see them on the news all the time. They had a little person, a real little person with life and spark and personality, and it's just...' she shook her head '...ripped from their grasp. One day they have a little boy or girl in their room at home, talking, laughing, playing, then the next day because of disease or accidents or war their precious little person is stolen from them. Gone, in the blink of an eye.'

Her eyes fixed on the uneven ground beneath their feet. 'That's when I think that most of the time I don't know what I missed. I can pretend.

I can build up all these thoughts of what Ariella Rose could have been like in my head.' She met his gaze. 'But the truth is, you and I will never know. Is it easier to lose a baby that you loved and hoped for than it is to lose an actual child you've spent years bringing up?' She shook her head again.

'I try to rationalise why I feel so empty. I try to make excuses about why I don't want to be around pregnant colleagues or friends.' She gave him a sad kind of smile. 'I have twelve years' worth of excuses, Logan, with reasons for not visiting new babies or friends playing happy families. It would surprise you how often I'm away with work.'

He could feel the tiny hairs standing up at the back of his neck. It just didn't feel quite right. He could feel her stepping back, detaching herself from the thoughts and feelings she'd been having a few moments ago. It was the slight change in the tone of her voice. The cool way she could look at him now.

For a few seconds her heart had been virtually on display. Her fears and hidden emotions had been coming to the surface. But even though she hadn't moved, was still sitting on the chair next to him, still letting their legs touch, she was pulling back again.

The only reason he could pick up on the tiny clues was because he knew her so well.

She straightened her spine in the chair. He could sense her sorting out her thoughts, finding a way to steal herself back from what she'd almost revealed.

He reached out to take her hand again. 'How would you feel about taking a visit to Florence again? How would you feel about us going together to Ariella Rose's grave?'

She pulled her hand back sharply from his, almost as if she'd been stung. It was too much. It was a step too far.

She wasn't ready to take it. She might never be ready to take it.

And with that realisation he felt the woman he'd always loved slip away from him once again.

Her face had turned into a mask. 'I don't want to do that, Logan. I don't think it's necessary.'

Her phone beeped in her bag and she bent forward, obviously glad of the distraction.

Their coffees and breakfast were virtually untouched, discarded.

A bit like how he felt right now.

She gave a false smile. 'It's work. With the computer program verifying Burano as the artist of the fresco, we can start to plan for the restoration now.'

She stood up quickly. It was almost as if their conversation had been forgotten.

For a few seconds he didn't move. He'd almost got there. *They'd* almost got there.

For him it was all or nothing. He knew that Lucia was the woman that he wanted, but he wasn't just prepared to accept a small part of her. And just when she'd started, just when she'd finally managed to talk about their daughter, it was almost as if he'd been able to see the shutters come down over her eyes, closing off the part of her that was most exposed, most vulnerable and cocooning it back in herself.

He had so many hidden hopes and plans for them. Last night had been wrong. Last night had made him think that there might just be hope for them. That this relationship could actually bloom and grow after all these years.

She didn't get it. She didn't get it that in his head they would grow old together. When they'd both lost their beauty, their youth and their health, they would still have each other. And that would be enough. That would always be enough.

Only it wasn't now. Not when he knew that the woman he loved with all his heart would never love him the same way. She couldn't. Part of her heart was permanently locked away. Had been for the last twelve years and it looked like it would stay that way for ever.

He stood up and put some notes on the table to cover breakfast. Lucia's whole face had changed. It was as if it had been replaced by a mask.

His stomach turned over. He could have played things so differently this morning. He could have ignored the past and just continued with the present, no matter how little of her he actually got.

But it would never have been enough. And

even though his heart felt as though she'd ripped it in two, he knew this was right. For him at least.

He kept his voice as detached as he could. He would never make a scene. Never do anything to deliberately cause her embarrassment or upset.

'Shall we make travel plans back to Tuscany?'

Her shoulders dropped a little as he spoke. Was that relief that he saw? Relief that he'd finally let things go?

Her words came out rapidly and her footsteps matched his on the cobbles next to the narrow canal. 'I can arrange the return flights. We should be able to go back first thing tomorrow morning. The samples that I took earlier will be sent for automatic colour and pigment matching. I can only restore the fresco using products as close to the originals as possible. Thank goodness for modern technology.' She gave a wave of her hand and kept chattering as they crossed the bridge.

Logan felt numb. This was it. This was it for him and her.

He'd have to spend the next few months in

Tuscany, working next to Lucia but keeping her at arm's length. Every glimpse whipped up a whole host of memories of the night before. He couldn't possibly be in her company and not think about what the two of them had lost and never recovered from.

There couldn't be a Logan and Lucia. Not if she still couldn't mourn their daughter.

It would be best for them both.

CHAPTER NINE

SHE FELT NUMB. It was the only way she could survive.

Last night had been a blur. They'd got up this morning just as the sun had been rising and made their way in a water taxi to the airport. Logan had spoken barely a word to her.

And that was what hurt most.

He'd been polite, of course, courteous even. But it had all been strained. Any time she'd caught a glimpse of his once gleaming green eyes all she'd been able to see was the blankness that had been pulled over them.

They stood patiently in the queue, checking in and filing through to Departures. As soon as they made their way through she made a feeble excuse that she needed to pick up some things.

Logan gave a nod of his head and said he was going for coffee and would meet her at the departure gate. He seemed almost as relieved as she was to get some space.

Lucia ducked into the nearest shop. She didn't even care which one it was—and started walking blankly through the aisles.

Lingerie. Just what she needed. She cringed as she passed a couple winking and nudging each other near the sexiest black and pink lingerie in the shop. She couldn't even remember the last time she'd spent money on matching lingerie. And she certainly wasn't going to need some any time soon. Not at these prices anyway. Who actually spent this kind of money on underwear?

Something inside her sparked a wave of fury. Her steps became quicker, more determined. She marched along the aisles until she saw something that caught her eye, something she might actually wear.

It was a pale pink satin nightdress trimmed with exquisite lace. It was not as short as she might usually wear, reaching down to at least her knees. She reached out and touched it. The heavy satin was silky to touch, pure of quality and luxury. She picked out her size and walked to the cashier's desk without a second thought.

The cashier folded and wrapped the nightdress in tissue paper and Lucia didn't even blink when she handed over her credit card.

Why shouldn't she buy herself something beautiful? As she pushed the package into her bag her mind flashed back to her bedroom and the beautiful red dress that Logan had bought her lying crumpled on the floor.

She hadn't even picked it up. She didn't need any reminder of the night they'd spent together. It was already ingrained in her brain.

She didn't need anything to remember the feel of his fingers on her skin, the feel of his lips on her neck and throat. The smell of his scent winding its way around her. The squeeze in her heart the next day when he'd told her they needed to talk.

And the look in his eyes when she'd finally stood up and walked away, pushing everything else back into a space she didn't have to deal with.

She'd been walking on eggshells ever since.

And not just around Logan. Around herself too.

For a few tiny seconds she allowed herself to think about Ariella Rose. She'd allowed herself to say a few words, to contemplate what might have been and what she'd lost.

But it had been too much. The wave of emotions that had swept over her had had to be quickly quelled. On that warm summer's day she'd never felt so cold. The tremors that had come over her body had been overwhelming.

It would have been so easy to bury her head in Logan's shoulder and just hold on for grim life. But she was too scared. Scared that if she went there she might never come back.

The truth was that no adult should outlive their child. And only someone who'd been there could understand that. Her friends and family had no idea of the type of thoughts that had crept through her brain in the few days after her daughter's death. She'd never acknowledged them to anyone.

Instead, she'd kept things locked away—even from Logan. How did you tell the man you loved with your whole heart that you would rather be with your daughter than him?

It had been too cruel. Even for her.

Her eyes scanned the coffee shop. Logan was sitting staring out of one of the windows, his hand stirring his cappuccino endlessly.

She dumped her bags in the chair next to him. It wouldn't be long until their flight was called. She walked over to the counter. 'Full-fat caramel latte with whipped cream and a strawberry frosted doughnut.'

A whole day's worth of calories about to be consumed in ten minutes. But she just felt like it. Sometimes days were just like that.

And from the look on Logan's face his day was entirely like that too.

It seemed the longest flight in history.

It was amazing the things you could think up to do rather than talk to the person sitting directly at your elbow.

Lucia was wearing a bright orange dress, and matching stilettos. She had a large brown leather bag—which looked as if it could carry the entire contents of her kitchen—slung over her shoulder.

Her wheeled suitcase looked bigger than his car. It was clear she was here to stay.

For a second he'd wondered if she was having second thoughts. She'd disappeared at the airport for a bit, then reappeared, eating a whole host of things that would never normally cross her lips.

Logan was far too wise to comment. Lucia hadn't been known for hormonal binges. But it had been twelve long years. Lots of things could have changed that he knew nothing about.

And, frankly, it wasn't his business any more.

As they landed at the private Tuscan airport and waited for their car, one of the signs at the newsstand caught his eye.

He gave her a nudge. *'When was the last time Prince Antonio saw his Cinderella bride?'*

For the first time since they'd left Venice the glazed expression left Lucia's face and her eyes widened. 'What on earth have we missed? We've only been gone a few days.'

He shook his head as the car pulled up in front

of them. 'I have no idea. We'll need to talk to Louisa as soon as we reach the *palazzo*. I wonder if this will have implications for the wedding?'

He opened the door for Lucia and they climbed inside. After a few seconds she pulled out her laptop and started working. Logan sighed and leaned back, watching the green Tuscan hills roll by.

The journey from the airport took them back through the village and he took a few moments to study the surrounding architecture again. It was important that he keep the *palazzo* as in keeping with its surroundings as possible. Any kind of modern renovation would be disastrous. So, while modern fixtures and fittings could be included, they had to be sympathetic to the history of the house.

They pulled up outside the *palazzo*. It was a hive of activity. Monday mornings in the Italian building trade could notoriously start slowly. Not today.

Connor was in talks with someone outside the

chapel building. It was obvious he was keeping on top of the security of the fresco.

A delivery of the special pink-coloured stone used in the *palazzo* was being unloaded. Some of the outer restoration work still needed to be completed. He could see his special stonemason signing for the delivery.

Louisa came walking out of the main entrance as Lucia grabbed her case. Louisa looked distracted, as if her mind were on a hundred other things. She hadn't even noticed their return.

'Louisa?' he said, trying to be heard above the building work around them. She was frowning and it marred her pretty face. Her hair was pulled back in a rumpled knot and her long tunic looked like yesterday's.

Her head flicked up. 'Logan.' Her eyes darted over to Lucia. 'Lucia. You're both back.' She walked over quickly. 'Do you have news?'

Lucia gave her a cautious smile. 'We do. The fresco *is* by Burano, he lived and worked in the Renaissance period and we have other examples of his work. He was both a painter and a sculptor. We're making arrangements to look at the sculpture on the fountain in the village. It could be another piece of his work.'

Louisa gave a smile and a quick nod. 'That's great. Really great. What happens next?'

Lucia glanced towards Logan. It was obvious that she was picking up the same vibes that he was. Louisa's body language was all over the place. She was saying the right words but her hands were continually knotting in front of her abdomen.

'Things will be fine. I'll begin the restoration work on the fresco. It could take a few months. All the costs will be covered by the Italian Heritage Board.'

'A few months?' Louisa looked shocked. 'But what about—?'

Logan stepped forward and took her arm, cutting her off. 'Are you okay? Don't worry about Lucia's work. It won't interfere with any of the plans here.' He nodded towards Lucia. 'We'll make sure of that.' He lowered his voice. 'Is this about the headlines? We saw them when we landed at the airport. Is the wedding still going ahead? Is there anything you need to tell us?'

Louisa's face tightened and she pressed her lips together. 'Of course the wedding is still going ahead. There's nothing to tell. Nothing to tell at all.'

It was clear by the tone of her voice that she wasn't willing to discuss anything.

She waved her hand towards the *palazzo*. 'Lucia, you're welcome to stay here, but...' she glanced at Lucia's stuffed suitcase '...you might need to make other arrangements while the wedding is taking place.'

Logan turned and stared at Lucia just as she turned and stared at him. Both of them had wide eyes. It was like a cartoon scene. It was something that hadn't occurred to either of them.

Of course Lucia would need somewhere to stay for the next few months. He'd invited her to stay with him in the farmhouse, but that had been when they'd been at the top of the campanile. It seemed like a million years ago. She'd promised to consider it and they hadn't discussed it again since.

He knew that he should say something here.

Logan's arrangement was different from everyone else's. He was staying in one of the old converted farmhouses on the estate. It was comfortable. It was private. And it was big enough for two people.

There were two reasonable-sized bedrooms. He had hardly set foot in the other one—even though he could have used it as his office. His computer and paperwork were currently spread over the dining-room table. Dining for one didn't really require the full use of the table.

He caught a glimpse of the expression on Louisa's face. She was caught in the middle, probably unable to fathom out what their relationship was. She waved her hand. 'I'll leave that to you two.' She walked away into the vineyards.

Lucia was watching her retreating back. 'Do you think she's okay?'

He shrugged. 'She certainly didn't want to be drawn into any gossip. She could be worried about how this could affect the prospects for the vineyard and the *palazzo*. I can only assume that the wedding costs are covering all the renovations around here. If they back out now...' He let his voice drift off. They both knew exactly what that could mean for Louisa.

Lucia gave a little nod and tugged at her case. 'In that case, I have things I need to do. I'm going back to chart some of the fresco and make an approximate estimate of how long the restoration work will take. I'll share the timetable with you when it's finished.'

Logan looked around. There was a mountain of work here for him too. A little gust of wind swept past and carried Lucia's rose-scented perfume towards him.

He cringed as it automatically evoked memories in his brain. Nights. Days. Passion. Love. And loss.

Avoiding Lucia in Palazzo di Comparino could be harder than he'd thought.

It could be nigh on impossible.

'See you later,' he said briskly as her eyes met his.

For the tiniest second he held his breath. There it was again, that connection. It sparked every time he looked into those deep brown eyes and reflected the pain and passion that had affected them both.

He dug his hands in his pockets and turned away.

It was best to break the connection.

Best for them both.

Lucia couldn't sleep. The windows in her bedroom were open wide and she could practically hear the music of the Tuscan hills calling to her. Every rustle of the vineyard leaves, every noise from the watering system, the tiny cranking noises of some of the mechanical systems were all being carried in the warm night air.

The bed was comfortable, but even wearing just her new satin nightdress and only having one sheet was proving too much. She couldn't settle. Every time she closed her eyes for a few seconds her brain started to replay the last few days with Logan.

And it was infuriating. Because it wasn't one tiny part—it was everything...almost told in parts like a TV series. Her nerves at speaking to him for the first time. That *whoosh* that had swept over her body when she'd set eyes on him again. The way her skin had prickled just from being near him. Feeling the heat from his body when he was in close proximity to her. The touch of his lips on hers, awakening all the old sensations. Being held in his arms as they'd danced at Piazza San Marco. And the feel of his skin against hers when they'd finally gone to bed together.

Being around Logan seemed to have set all of her five senses on fire. And now they'd been reawakened it seemed they didn't want to go back to sleep.

She sat up in bed for the twentieth time and slid her feet onto the floor. The tiles of the floor were cool and it took a few seconds to find her flat sandals.

She stood at the window for a moment, wondering if she should go outside. There was not a single person in sight. That wasn't unusual—it was the middle of the night. She glanced around her room.

There was somewhere she wanted to be. Was it worth getting changed? The chapel was only across the courtyard from the *palazzo*. Could she just sneak across the way she was?

She grimaced at the stuffed-full suitcase. Packing when your mind was on other things wasn't exactly ideal. She hadn't brought a dressing gown. Or her running gear. Or a hairdryer.

She opened her door. It creaked loudly and she held her breath for a few seconds to see if anyone had noticed the noise.

The air in the corridor was still. Her sandals made barely a sound as she crept along and down the stairs. The front door of the *palazzo* wasn't even locked.

She slipped outside and her footsteps quickened as she crossed the courtyard, the warm air making her nightdress flutter around her. It didn't matter, there was nobody to see her. She couldn't explain it. Couldn't even think about it too much. But she was being drawn to the chapel like a magnet.

Except it wasn't really the chapel she wanted to see—it was the fresco.

The thick wooden door was heavy and she had to put her shoulder to it to finally push it open.

The slightly colder, stiller air of the chapel swept around her as soon as she stepped inside. Her footsteps stopped as the tiny hairs on her arms stood upright.

It was like walking into a scene from a scary movie. She was being ridiculous. Of course the chapel was slightly colder. The walls were thicker than the *palazzo*'s and the cooler air had probably helped with the preservation of the fresco.

It was pitch-black. Only a few strands of moonlight were sneaking through the stained-glass windows. Nothing was really visible. She hadn't thought to bring a candle with her.

She took a few small steps forward, hoping her eyes would adjust to the darkness around her. Her hand reached out to touch the cold wall. It was odd. This chapel must have hundreds of years' worth of history, hundreds of years' worth of stories to tell. Weddings, birth, funerals all held in here.

In a way it was nice the royal wedding was being held here. A piece of history was being brought back to life, back to its former glory. If they hadn't proposed to use this site, Burano's fresco might never have been discovered.

'Yaow!' She stubbed her foot on something—some kind of carpenter's toolbox—and bent to rub her bare toe. Her hand touched something on the floor. She fumbled for a second. A flashlight. Perfect. She flicked the switch and a thin beam of light cut through the darkness.

Now she could move more easily. She spun the torch around towards the fresco wall, the light hitting squarely on the Madonna's face. Lucia sucked in a breath. Her feet moved forward automatically. An invisible hand had reached into her chest and was squeezing at her heart.

This was it. This was what she'd needed to see. She moved the light a little downwards onto the face of baby Jesus, then back towards Mary. She drew up directly to the fresco, her hand shaking a little as Mary's face was illuminated in all its glory.

Every hint of colour, every hair on her head, every tiny line of her face—it was the expression that had been captured so beautifully. The expression that made her knees tremble.

She'd never seen it captured quite so perfectly. Even though it was paint that was centuries old she felt as if she could reach out and touch Mary. Stroke her cheek, feel the warmth of her skin, see the wonder in her eyes.

This was what she'd remembered. It was the thing that she'd pushed to the back of her head when she'd first seen the fresco. Now it was drawing her back.

Now she couldn't deny it. She couldn't ignore it.

This had all been in Burano's imagination. It felt as if he'd stepped back in time and caught that moment when a mother first looked at her child and was overcome by that huge wave of emotions and undeniable love. Baby Jesus was looking back at his mother with childlike wonder and awe. The look of love that only a child could give his mother—making the bond complete. The light behind the depiction of the Madonna and Child was almost ethereal. The glow around them was all-encompassing. All-consuming.

Her legs trembled. Her whole body was shaking.

And something, something from deep inside, was pushing its way out.

This was what she had missed. This was what she'd missed out on. This was what would never be hers. Never be shared between her and her daughter.

Her legs gave way, collapsing beneath her onto the dusty chapel floor as the sobs started to come out.

And twelve years' worth of suppressed grief started to flow.

Logan was pacing. He hadn't even made an attempt to go to bed. He'd heard rustling in the vineyard and had taken a restless walk to investigate. It had been fruitless. He'd found nothing. It had probably only been a fox.

But as he had been crossing back towards his farmhouse, something had caught his eye. At first he'd thought he had finally gone crazy and was imagining it. Then he'd looked again.

Lucia. Dressed in very little with bare legs, bare arms and a pale pink lace-trimmed nightdress fluttering around her in the warm breeze and clinging to every curve of her skin. Was she sleepwalking?

She seemed so focused, so light on her feet, that she almost floated across the courtyard, straight to the chapel entrance. He'd started to move in her direction but his footsteps had faltered as she'd paused at the chapel door, pushing it with her shoulder to lever it open.

Then she disappeared into the darkness.

Logan stopped. His heart was thudding in his chest. Should he follow, or should he leave?

Every part of his rational brain told him to step away. No matter how much he wanted to, he couldn't pursue a relationship with Lucia. Not like this. Not when they were both in different places.

But the protective element in him couldn't walk away. Couldn't leave her like this.

He walked quietly towards the chapel. A little beam of light appeared inside the chapel, cutting across the stained-glass windows. What was she doing?

He held his breath as he reached the doorway. Stepping inside the dark chapel was intimidating—and he was fully dressed. The thin beam of torchlight was focused on the fresco on the faraway wall.

He'd never seen it lit up like this before. He'd only ever really studied it in daylight. It looked entirely different under the concentrated light of a torch beam. The architect-minded part of him wondered how it must have looked hundreds of years ago in flickering candlelight.

Lucia had the beam directly on the Madonna's face. Under the artificial light her face was brightly illuminated. In a reach-out-and-touch kind of way.

The beam wobbled and he stepped forward. Part of his stomach was curled up in a ball. Lucia had come out to the chapel in the middle of the night. In the light reflected back off the fresco he could see her trembling, shuddering skin. Every muscle, every bone was shaking.

His response was automatic. He stepped forward just as she crumpled to the floor, her sobs cutting through the night air. The torch fell to the floor with a crash, the light sputtering out.

He was stunned. In twelve years he hadn't

heard her cry. There had been a few tears just after the birth of their daughter—but none after that.

He wrapped his arms around her. Her skin was cold, chilled in the coolness of the chapel, so he pulled her against his chest and stroked her hair. He didn't care about the dust. He didn't care about the broken torch on the ground.

He just held her.

And she sobbed. Like no one he'd ever heard before. These weren't quiet, tiny sobs. These were loud and spluttering, echoing around the thick chapel walls. Her body was racked with them and he could feel her pain, feel her anguish. It was as if twelve years' worth of grief and sorrow had just erupted from her soul.

It was horrible to see the woman he loved like this. But he knew exactly how she felt. Only he could understand. So he waited and he held her, gently stroking her hair and whispering in her ear.

He had no idea how long they stayed that way. Eventually her sobs quietened, turning into little shudders instead of big outbursts. He changed position, pulling her up onto his knees, taking her bare legs away from the cold floor of the chapel.

His hands sneaked around her satin-covered waist and he pulled her against his chest. Her hands snaked up around his neck and her head tucked under his chin. He could feel her ragged breaths against his skin.

'I know, Lucia,' he said softly. 'I know how you feel. I loved her just as much as you did.'

She gave a little whimper and her fingers tightened around his neck. He waited a few seconds then gently lifted her head up. There was only a tiny bit of moonlight streaming through the stained-glass windows but he could see her tear-streaked face and he lifted both hands to caress it.

'Talk to me,' he whispered.

She shuddered, then nodded slowly.

It was odd. The strangest feeling in the world, but it was almost as if his body gave a little cry of relief.

'I miss her,' she said in shaky breaths. 'I miss her every day.'

His heart squeezed in his chest. He wanted to wrap his arms around her again and kiss her. But he needed to let her speak.

'I don't want to talk about her,' she said, her voice tinged with regret. 'If I don't talk about her, then none of it was real. None of it really happened.'

She shook her head as her voice rose in pain. 'Why, Logan? Why our baby? Why did we have to lose her? Do you know where we could be right now? Do you know what kind of life we could be leading?'

He nodded his head. 'Of course I do,' he whispered.

'But you were so calm, so controlled,' she said angrily. 'I couldn't be like that, I just couldn't. You did everything. You organised the flowers, the funeral, the casket. You spoke to the family.' She shook her head, her voice rising. 'How could you even do that? How could you even function? Our daughter was dead!'

'You think I didn't know that? You think I didn't hurt every bit as much as you? I hated that, Lucia. I hated every second of that. I hated the fact you wouldn't eat, you wouldn't sleep and you wouldn't talk to me. Organising was the only thing I *could* do. I wanted the world to know that Ariella Rose had existed. I wanted her to matter. I wanted to bury our daughter with the respect she deserved.' He hadn't realised this had been buried inside him. He hadn't realised he'd wanted to say all this to her.

'And I didn't?' She was crying again. 'You were so…capable. And I felt useless. I couldn't be the person I'd been. I couldn't be your other half. I couldn't look at you without thinking about her and what had been stolen from me!'

He clasped her head between his hands and leaned his forehead against hers. 'Stolen from *us*, Lucia,' he said quietly.

'I needed you. I needed you every second of the day. But I couldn't get to you. You locked yourself away from me and after a few weeks I realised that you needed to grieve differently from me. I didn't want to let you go. I never wanted to let you go. No matter how sorry I was, no matter how much I hurt, I still wanted you, Lucia. Every second of every day. You're the only person in this world for me. The only person I want to grow old with.' He traced a finger down her damp cheek. 'I just needed to see you cry. I just needed to know that you could acknowledge our daughter.'

She was still shuddering. He ran one hand down her arm and could feel the tiny hairs on her arms standing on end.

'Why now? What's changed?'

She met his gaze with tear-filled eyes. 'You. I've avoided you for so long. Seeing you again, being together, remembering everything we've shared together, I couldn't hide away from it any more. It's just been bubbling underneath the surface the whole time. I couldn't keep it locked away any more. Not if I want to live.'

He gave his head a shake. 'But you wouldn't talk to me in Venice. You said you couldn't do it.'

She squeezed her eyes closed for a moment. 'I know.' Now she reached up and touched his face, his jaw. 'I think something just lined up for us, Logan.' She pointed towards the fresco. 'If you hadn't got this job, if this fresco hadn't been found, we probably wouldn't have met again.' She placed her hand over her heart. 'I *needed* this. I needed all this to happen.' She looked up towards the fresco. 'Hundreds of years ago Burano must have met someone, must have known a new mother, to capture the love and adoration in his painting. Because he's captured it so beautifully. When I first saw his fresco I wouldn't let the painting touch me. I wouldn't let it inside. I was jealous. I couldn't acknowledge the painting because *I* wanted to be that person. *I* wanted to be that mother who looks at her baby with such joy and pleasure, wondering what the world will hold for them.' The tears were falling freely down her face again.

All he wanted to do was comfort her. All he wanted to do was love her.

He sucked in a deep breath. 'Lucia, you can be that person. I want you to know that I love you. I want you—just the way you are. But if you want to try and have a family again then I'll be with you, every step of the way.' He stroked his thumb across her cheek. 'Likewise, if you just want to grow old and grey together and wander through the streets of Venice, or Florence, or even the Tuscan hills, I'll do that with you too. As long as I'm with you, I know I'll be happy.'

Her hands kept trembling as she wound them around his neck again, pressing her body against his and whispering in his ear. 'Can I be enough for you, Logan? Enough for you on my own? What if we weren't meant to have babies? What if that's never going to happen for us?'

He stood up, pulling her to her feet alongside him but keeping their bodies locked close together. He slid his hands along the satin slip covering her back and anchored her to him. He kissed one cheek and then the other. 'Then that's the way things are supposed to be. As long as I'm with you I can take whatever hand life deals us.'

He bent to meet her lips.

It was like the first kiss all over again.

This was the woman he'd fallen in love with all those years ago.

This was the woman he'd had to allow to walk away even though it had broken his heart.

This was the mother of his child.

This was his Lucia.

Her body was pressed against his and she responded to every touch, her fingers threading through his hair. Her rose scent wound around him, pulling him in in every way.

Her cold skin heated quickly, her lips matching every kiss.

For Logan, it was like coming home.

When Lucia finally pulled back he was shocked. She lifted a finger and placed it against his lips, keeping her body tight against his.

She took a deep breath. 'Logan, if this is going to work, there's something I need to do.'

His breath was caught somewhere in his throat. After twelve years there was finally a chance of a relationship again with Lucia. There wasn't anything he wouldn't agree to.

'What is it? What do you need to do? Because I don't want to lose you again. I don't want this chance to slip away from us.'

Her voice was trembling and her hand slid down his arm, interlocking their fingers. 'I was kind of hoping you would agree to do it with me.'

Her dark eyes met his gaze and he squeezed her hand tightly. 'Anything, Lucia,' he whispered. 'Anything for you.'

CHAPTER TEN

IT WAS A gorgeous summer's day with the sun high in the sky above them.

Logan was standing in front of her in his trademark cream suit and pale blue shirt. 'Ready?' he asked.

Her stomach was churning. Over and over. She would have tossed and turned last night if he hadn't held her safely in his arms. She'd even bought herself a new dress. Pale pink with tiny flowers. It was ridiculous. She didn't need it. But she'd wanted to wake up this morning and feel like everything was new.

More than anything, she wanted to be prepared.

Florence was alive. She'd forgotten how much she loved this city. Chattering voices were all around them, tourist parties bustling past and

Italian voices mixing with a multitude of other languages.

She slid her hand into his, clutching her pink and lilac flowers in her hand. 'I'm ready,' she said with a certainty she hadn't known she possessed.

The walk through the streets took around fifteen minutes, the crowds lessening the further out they went. No one else was going where they were.

It was a pleasant walk with a few shopkeepers nodding at Logan as they passed by and him pointing out a few changes to the city since she'd left.

As the green archway of the cemetery came into view her footsteps faltered. Logan slipped his hand around her waist. As their bodies pressed against each other she fell into step with him. It felt natural and gave her the added reassurance to continue.

The cemetery was quiet, bathed in warm sunlight, with only a few people dotted around in quiet condolence.

Her throat was closing up as they walked along

the white paved path. Like most cemeteries this one had a special section for children and babies. It was tucked away at the back, next to the white wall that separated the cemetery from the rest of the city.

There was a white bench in the middle, with lots of green grass and flower beds erupting with colour. Something inside her clenched. She hadn't allowed herself to think about this. She hadn't allowed herself to realise the beauty of the surroundings.

Within the cemetery walls she couldn't even hear the noise of the city outside. It was like their own private sanctuary.

She squeezed her eyes closed as they passed rows of little white headstones. So many little lives lost. So many other people who'd experienced the same pain that she had.

Had she maybe even met some of them? She'd been so immersed in her own grief that she hadn't stopped to think about anyone else's.

Their footsteps slowed. She'd only been here once and Logan had been numerous times but she still knew exactly where Ariella Rose was buried—it was imprinted in her brain.

They stopped and stood for a second, looking down at the little white headstone.

Beloved daughter.
Ariella Rose Cascini.
Born asleep.

Apart from the date, there was nothing else on the stone.

Lucia laid her head on his shoulder as silent tears fell down her cheeks. She needed this. She'd needed to do this for so long.

A dove swooped in the air above them, landing on the grass at their feet. Lucia gave a little nod of her head as it eyed her suspiciously then walked away. She put her pale pink and lilac flowers into the little white vase at the graveside then leaned over to touch the stone.

It was odd. Any marble headstone she'd ever touched before had been cold. But Ariella's wasn't. It was bathed in the bright light and warmed by the sun.

The horrible closed-in feeling that had been

around her heart for so long was gone. The terrible weight and the dark cloud that had pressed on her shoulders for the last twelve years was finally gone.

Today she didn't feel despair all around her. Today she saw a beautiful memorial and resting place for her darling daughter. A place where she could come and sit sometimes if she needed to.

She'd been so afraid for so long. But with Logan by her side she didn't need to be.

'I love you, Ariella Rose,' she whispered. 'I'm sorry I haven't been here and I promise to visit in the future.' She stroked her hand along the stone and stood up, taking the few steps to Logan and wrapping her arms around his waist.

'Thank you,' she said quietly. 'Thank you for bringing me here.'

'Any time. Any time at all.'

He threaded his fingers back through hers. 'Do you want to take some time? How do you feel?' His voice was cautious.

She tilted her head up towards the sun and the

face of the man that she loved and adored. The man she wanted to grow old with.

'I feel as if I've taken that step. The one that I've needed to for so long. I'm ready now.'

He clasped both her hands in his. 'Ready for what?'

She met the gaze of his steady green eyes. 'Ready to move forward. Now I can love the man I want to without feeling overcome with grief.' She smiled up at the sun. 'Now I can look towards the future.'

There was a swell in her chest. A confidence she hadn't felt in so long.

He reached up and slid his hand through her hair as he pulled her to him.

'Then let's start now.'

And he kissed her.

And she kissed him right back.

She was laughing. She was running through the cobbled streets of Monte Calanetti in her impossibly high heels.

He loved it. He loved every second of it. 'Watch out!' he shouted. 'You'll break something!'

'Keep up, slowcoach!' she shouted over her shoulder as she made the final dash towards the fountain. He walked up behind her and slid his hands around her waist. He could feel her rapid breaths against his chest wall.

'Do you have them?' she asked.

He unfurled his fingers, revealing the shiny euro coins in his hand. He eyed the clamshell the nymph held above her head in the centre of the fountain. 'First time?' He was smiling. She'd tried this a hundred times before and had never managed to hit the mark—the clamshell that would make your wish come true.

Her deep brown eyes met his. 'First time,' she repeated. Her index finger moved the coins in the palm of his hand as if she was looking for just the right one. After a few seconds she smiled. 'This one,' she said, weighing the coin in her hand.

'That one? You're sure?'

'Oh, I'm sure.' She spun around to face the nymph. His hand was on her abdomen and she pressed her right hand over his, as she took a deep breath, pulled back her left hand and let the coin fly.

His eyes stayed on the coin as it caught the sunlight as it arced through the air, but his left hand was flicking something else into the fountain at their feet.

The coin was on a direct path and landed squarely in the middle of the clamshell. Lucia let out a shriek. 'I've done it! I've finally done it!' She spun around and flung her arms around his neck. 'I've finally done it.'

He picked her up and spun her around, her hair streaming out behind her. 'You've done it,' he cheered as he set her back down. 'Now, what did you wish for?'

For the first time his stomach wasn't in knots around Lucia. Slowly but surely she was turning back into the woman he loved. The dark shadows were going from her eyes. Her steps were lighter. She laughed more. She cried more. And she still loved to dance.

'Isn't the wish supposed to be a secret?' she said coyly.

He swallowed. He'd never felt more nervous,

or surer about anything in his life. 'Look down,' he said quietly.

She blinked. It obviously wasn't what she had expected to hear. A frown creased her brow as she stared down, taking a few seconds to see the glint of gold under the clear water.

Her eyes widened and she bent down, putting her hand into the water and pulling out the ring.

'Logan?' she asked as a smile spread across her face.

It wasn't a traditional flashy engagement ring. He didn't want to waste any time. It was a gold wedding band studded with diamonds and rubies. It was a ring of promise. A ring of hope.

He didn't hesitate, just got down on one knee in front of the woman he loved. 'Lucia Moretti. You're the woman of my dreams. The woman I love with my whole heart. You are my perfect match. The person I want to laugh with, cry with, play with and grow old with. I believe this was meant to happen. I honestly believe we were meant to meet again and mourn our daughter together. I don't care where you want to make a life. I don't care if it's Venice, Florence, Rome or anywhere else. All that matters to me is that home is with you.' He pressed his hand against his heart. 'As long as I'm with you, I don't care where we are. You're the person I call home. You're all that I need. Will you make me the happiest man alive and marry me?'

She was still staring at the ring, watching the sun glint off the little diamonds and rubies. The smile was permanently etched on her face.

She wrapped one arm around his neck and sat down on his knee. She didn't hesitate to slip the ring on her finger. 'How on earth could any woman refuse such a romantic proposal at Burano's fountain?' Her eyes were twinkling. She put her hand over his. 'There's no one else I ever want to be with. You're the only man for me.'

He pulled something out from behind his waist. 'I've brought you something else.'

She stared at the wrapped package. It wasn't big, small enough to tuck into his waistband. Plain canvas tied with string. She pulled the string and let the package unfurl. It was new paintbrushes and some oils. Her mouth fell open.

'How…how did you know?'

'That you'd want to take up painting again?'

She nodded as her eyes glistened with tears. 'Because we've come such a long way, Lucia. We've both moved on. You used to love painting and I know that you've found that little piece in your heart again that makes you ready to start again.'

She nodded her head slowly. 'You're right. I have. But I'd only just started to think about it.' She looked around. 'We're in such beautiful surroundings I can't help but feel inspired.'

He leaned forward to kiss her. 'Which leads me to my next question. Where do you want to live?'

She smiled and looked around. 'This might surprise you, but I've kind of grown fond of these Tuscan hills. I like the peace. I like the quiet. Maybe I'm not the city girl I thought.' She bit her bottom lip. 'How would you feel about finding somewhere to live around here?'

He stood and pulled her to her feet, holding her close. He ran his fingers through her hair. 'I think that this is a good place, a healing place. And I'm sure there's a Tuscan villa somewhere in these hills just waiting for us to renovate it. A villa where we can build you your own studio.'

She smiled again, 'All work and no play makes Logan a dull boy.'

She was teasing and he knew it. 'Who says anything about working?' he murmured.

She pressed a little kiss against his lips. 'Do you want to know what I wished for?'

'Are you going to tell me?'

She nodded. 'Someone must have been listening. When I threw that coin I wished for new beginnings.'

His eyebrows rose. 'You did?' It was perfect. It was as if everything was just meant to be.

'I did,' she said with confidence, and with that she rose up on her toes to kiss him. 'To new beginnings,' she whispered.

'New beginnings,' he murmured, and he kissed her right back.

* * * * *

MILLS & BOON®
Large Print – March 2016

A Christmas Vow of Seduction
Maisey Yates

Brazilian's Nine Months' Notice
Susan Stephens

The Sheikh's Christmas Conquest
Sharon Kendrick

Shackled to the Sheikh
Trish Morey

Unwrapping the Castelli Secret
Caitlin Crews

A Marriage Fit for a Sinner
Maya Blake

Larenzo's Christmas Baby
Kate Hewitt

His Lost-and-Found Bride
Scarlet Wilson

Housekeeper Under the Mistletoe
Cara Colter

Gift-Wrapped in Her Wedding Dress
Kandy Shepherd

The Prince's Christmas Vow
Jennifer Faye

0216 Rom LP

MILLS & BOON®
Large Print – April 2016

The Price of His Redemption
Carol Marinelli

Back in the Brazilian's Bed
Susan Stephens

The Innocent's Sinful Craving
Sara Craven

Brunetti's Secret Son
Maya Blake

Talos Claims His Virgin
Michelle Smart

Destined for the Desert King
Kate Walker

Ravensdale's Defiant Captive
Melanie Milburne

The Best Man & The Wedding Planner
Teresa Carpenter

Proposal at the Winter Ball
Jessica Gilmore

Bodyguard...to Bridegroom?
Nikki Logan

Christmas Kisses with Her Boss
Nina Milne

MILLS & BOON®

Why shop at millsandboon.co.uk?

Each year, thousands of romance readers find their perfect read at millsandboon.co.uk. That's because we're passionate about bringing you the very best romantic fiction. Here are some of the advantages of shopping at www.millsandboon.co.uk:

* **Get new books first**—you'll be able to buy your favourite books one month before they hit the shops

* **Get exclusive discounts**—you'll also be able to buy our specially created monthly collections, with up to 50% off the RRP

* **Find your favourite authors**—latest news, interviews and new releases for all your favourite authors and series on our website, plus ideas for what to try next

* **Join in**—once you've bought your favourite books, don't forget to register with us to rate, review and join in the discussions

Visit **www.millsandboon.co.uk**
for all this and more today!